The Artist's Adventure

Ashley Mechling

THE ARTIST'S ADVENTURE

Copyright © 2025 by Ashley Mechling
All rights reserved. No part of this book may be reproduced in any manner whatsoever without written permission except in the case of brief quotations embodied in critical articles and reviews.
First Printing, 2025

1

Chapter 1

I've lived in several places throughout my life. Always moving from one place to the next. Why should New York be any different from the rest? I thought to myself.

I unbuckled my seatbelt as my mom pulled into the driveway of our new home. It was a single floor home, nothing special. The outside was a faded shade of light blue with off white trim that was peeling in more places than not.

I hopped out of the passenger seat of the mover's truck and walked around the back to lift open the back door. I handed my mom one of the smaller boxes and followed her to the front door with another one. We walked into the front entrance, which opened to the living room and kitchen. I turned on the light switch and paused for a moment, taking in a deep breath, observing the space in front of me. It was dry, plain, and quiet. I carried my box to the back end of the house where my bedroom was. The walls were painted a light shade of grey, a stream of sunlight glowed across the space from a window on the other side of the room. I set the box down and scanned the small room, letting out a deep sigh.

I guess this is my new room, I thought to myself. *How charming.*

I helped my mom carry in the rest of the boxes before the sun set. We unboxed in the kitchen, which didn't take long. We didn't have that many dishes. My mom hated to cook, and I hated eating the food she tries and fails to make. We usually live off takeout or small meals I can make.

"I think I'll order some pizza," my mom announced, pulling her light brown, curly hair up into a bun. I nodded back and moved the empty boxes out of the room. We moved on to unboxing my mom's art supplies in the living room. My mom liked to use the open space as her art studio, making sculptures out of clay.

We'd moved from state to state all my life, trying to sell her artwork to various dealers. Her dream was to open her own art studio and for me to run it with her. I admired her dream and planned on helping her achieve it, but I don't see it happening anytime soon. She loved adventure and wasn't one to settle or plant roots, making it hard for her to achieve her dreams.

We finished our pizza and headed to our rooms for the night. I shut the door behind me and climbed into bed, looking around at all the boxes left to unpack and let out a sigh. I dreaded the thought of going through all of them. Most of the boxes are filled with paint supplies and artwork of my own. I hoped to become a famous painter one day with a successful studio. It was a pipe dream probably but still, something to live for.

I awoke the next morning to the sound of my alarm ringing in my ears. I moaned as I reached for my phone to shut it off. I groaned and rolled out of bed, wrapping myself in my black, fuzzy robe. I shuffled out of my room and into the bathroom across the hall. I took a fast shower, dreading the day. I was starting my first day at my new high school. It was the middle of the semester with graduation around the corner. Being the new girl never gets old, and with only two months left, that left me no time to make friends.

I wrapped myself in a towel, combing out my wet, dark, cherry red hair. I blow-dried my hair straight and brushed my teeth, finishing my morning routine by applying some light and natural makeup. I headed out to the kitchen to find my mom making coffee.

"Sleep, okay?" she asked.

"Eh, all right," I replied.

She gave me the look and handed me a mug filled to the brim. I gulped it down and grabbed a muffin as I turned to head out the front door.

"Play nice with the other kids!" my mom called after me.

I rolled my eyes and closed the door behind me. I unlocked my old, black, sedan and climbed into the driver's seat, tossing my violet bookbag onto the passenger seat. I started the ignition and linked my phone to Spotify, playing some alternative music as I pulled out of the driveway.

School was a fast ten-minute drive through the small streets of Beacon, New York. It was a quiet and small town that was far enough from Manhattan to escape the city.

I slowly pulled into the parking lot of the school. Groups of students walked toward the building. I pulled into a parking space next to a new, red Mustang. I paused before getting out of the car, observing the other students. They were all dressed in athletic clothing with the school's name spelled out across them. I felt the peppiness seeping out of the cheerleaders practicing a chant outside the front entrance.

I rolled my eyes and killed the ignition of my car and climbed out, throwing my backpack across my shoulders. I put on my black, square sunglasses and headed toward the front entrance. I walked through the front doors and felt judgmental eyes staring at me as I walked down the hall. Jocks from left to right, looking at me as the outsider I was. I lifted my chin, reflecting the florescent lights off my sunglasses, letting them know I didn't give a damn about their opinions.

I followed my schedule to my first two classes before I realized the room number for my third period class wasn't printed. I scoffed as I turned to head to the administrative office.

I walked into my guidance counselor's office and was greeted by a middle-aged woman with blonde hair and a pale blue sweater.

"Hello!" she greeted with an overly wide smile.

"Hi," I half smiled back. "Uh, I was following my schedule and saw the room number for my third period class didn't print." I said, sliding my schedule across her desk. She glanced over it quickly before seeing I was telling the truth. She printed me out a new one, inspecting that all the information was there before handing it to me.

"Thanks," I spoke and stood up to leave her office.

"Before you go," she announced. "Should we discuss the dress code while you're here?"

I looked at her confused and glanced down at my black jeans, white combat boots and black, lazy T-shirt.

"I don't see anything wrong with my clothes?" I questioned. She looked back at me with a fake smile.

"Well, the nose ring you have in isn't quite appropriate for a young girl like you, and you have so many studs in your ears. I can't imagine those are very comfortable," she said, gesturing toward me. "And you might want to wear some brighter colors. I'm sure you've noticed most of the students here wear nice, pressed clothing that supports our school's sports teams. Maybe you could try out for the volleyball team!" She exclaimed. "And your purple hair, it's a little too much, someone as young as you shouldn't be damaging your hair like that," she judged.

I let out a deep sigh, feeling my hands shake as I met her gaze.

"Maybe you should shove your prejudice for creative expression!" I shouted. I stormed out of the office, slamming the door behind me. I stepped back out into the hallway, staring at the never-ending display of classroom doors.

"Forget this," I muttered under my breath and turned to walk out a side door, out of the school. I took in a deep breath, feeling the cool air brush against my pale cheeks. I looked out onto a wooded area along the outskirts of the school. I glanced back at my car in the parking lot, debating on whether to run toward it. I took in another deep breath before taking a step toward the woods. *A walk through the trees should help me cool off,* I thought.

I stumbled through tree branches and ivy, almost tripping over myself several times. I instantly regretted my decision of going for a hike. I swatted at the leaves left and right, blowing my hair out of my face. I stepped forward through the brush, trapping my boot under a log and throwing myself forward, falling face first into a pile of dirt.

"Are you kidding me!" I yelled out, slamming my hands down and pushing myself up from the ground. I brought myself to my knees, wiping off my face with my sleeves and dusting off my hands when I heard a chuckle. I jumped out of skin and onto my feet. I turned around to find a dark-haired boy laughing at me.

"What're you doing here!?" I shouted at him. He lifted his gaze, looking back at me with bright blue eyes that shone against his dark brown, messy hair. He gave me an arrogant smirk and crossed his black sneaker across the knee of his black jeans.

"Same as you-I'm ditching." he replied coolly. I let out a sigh, feeling the relief lift from my shoulders.

"You don't look like the cliché jocks that fill that waste of a school," I observed. He let out a low belly laugh, slappy his hand on his thigh.

"Hell no, sports were never an interest. I would rather spend my time doing other things." He countered. "You don't look like you fit in with the in crowd either."

I looked him up and down, determining if he was as arrogant as he came off.

"No, I never have. I prefer to spend my time doing other things," I mocked.

He looked me deep in the eye, giving me a smirk. He bit his lip slightly before standing up on his feet. He straightened up his black T-shirt and threw his grey backpack over his shoulders.

"So, are you driving, or am I?" he questioned.

"Drive?" I asked. "Drive where?"

"Away from here, obviously. Anywhere but here." He gestured. I gazed at him cautiously, determining if I should trust this stranger who was hiding out in the woods alone or run screaming. Sensing my unease, he took a step forward, feeling my breath catch in my throat, I allowed him to stand closer to me. He raised his hand slowly, never leaving my gaze, he reached out toward my hair, running his fingers through it slowly, pulling out a twig that was caught. I felt my hands shake and my breathing become shallow and quick.

"Thank you," I whispered.

"So, are you driving? Or should I?" he replied softly.

"You should, probably," I spoke.

He smiled warmly and lead the way back out of the woods. I followed close behind, watching my step closely to ensure I didn't fall again.

We came out into the clearing, heading toward the parking lot. I followed behind him to an old, blue, Chevy Camaro convertible.

"This is yours?" I asked surprised.

"Yeah, I rebuilt the engine myself." he remarked while unlocking the doors.

We climbed inside, settling into the leather seats. The engine roared alive as he pulled out his phone and turned on some heavy rock music. I nodded in satisfaction and buckled my seatbelt. He drove out of the school parking lot, heading out onto the main road.

"So, what's your name, anyway? Mysterious girl with red hair," He smirked.

I rolled my eyes and looked out the window before replying. "Luna, my name is Luna." I mocked, looking back at him. "And what's your name? Angsty and arrogant boy?"

He let out a loud chuckle. "Eric, my name is Eric." He laughed.

I gazed out at the scenery passing by, greenery everywhere and a bright blue sky. I let out a deep sigh, relaxing my shoulders and leaning my head against the side of the car.

"So, where are we going anyway?" I questioned.

"I figured I'd show you the Hudson Beach Glass, I think you'll like it," he answered.

"Sounds interesting." I perked up. "What is it?" I asked.

"You'll find out when we get there, he smirked.

I rolled my eyes back at him and listened to the music that filled the air between us. I rolled down my window slightly, inviting the wind to flow against my cheeks. The fresh air filled my lungs and for the first time all day, I wasn't angry.

We arrived at the surprise location and parked the car. We walked up to an old brick building that stood overshadowing us. Eric opened the front door, and I stepped inside to an open room lined with endless countertops and tables filled with glass blown fixtures. I stopped in my tracks, inhaling a shard gasp.

"Oh, my, God." I replied, astonished. "This is amazing!"

I stepped forward slowly, approaching a display table. I gently reached out, slowly picking up a glass blown ornament. I held it up to the light, it glowed luminously in golden and red monochromatic colors.

"Beautiful," I exhaled.

I turned to find Eric watching me. I looked away quickly, trying to hide the red heat rising in my cheeks. I put down the fixture and walked around the store, gazing at the other art.

"So, are you from Beacon?" I asked Eric.

"Unfortunately." he replied. "But I plan on moving to Colorado and living in the mountains. I've always admired the atmosphere out there." he admitted.

"Wow, Colorado. I've never been," I confessed. "I've lived in many places but not there. When do you plan on moving?" I asked.

"Soon, I was thinking this summer, after graduation. Unless something changes my mind," he responded.

I stopped and glanced over my shoulder back at him. He gazed into my eyes with a deep longing. I broke the tension and looked away sheepishly.

"But won't you miss your family here?" I countered.

"No." He spoke bluntly. He cleared his throat before replying softly again. "No, I won't miss my family here. Except for my younger sister, Anna. She's a freshman at the high school," he explained.

I paused, hesitant on whether to further this conversation. "Are you two very close?" I asked.

"Not very, you know how siblings are. But I do look out for her," he replied.

I nodded in understanding.

We finished up observing the art and headed back out to the car. We hopped inside and pulled back out on to the street.

"I should probably be heading home. I'm sure my mom is wondering where I went after the school called," I spoke.

"You're lucky," he expressed. "To have a mom who worries."

"Does your mom not worry about you?" I asked.

Eric shifted in his seat, gripping the steering wheel.

"I'm sorry, I didn't mean to ask something so personal." I apologized, feeling guilty.

"Don't worry about it," he replied, glancing at me. "No harm done."

We arrived back at the school's parking lot, pulling up next to my car. He put the car in park before shifting toward me.

"Should we meet back at the tree stump tomorrow?" He questioned.

I smiled and turned toward him.

"I guess I can manage that. But it'll have to be after school lets out, I can't ditch again," I teased.

"Far enough," he agreed. We looked at each for a moment in silence, memorizing each other's faces. Every line, every freckle, the fine details of their eyes. Eric leaned in slowly, pausing for a moment, glancing at my lips, before leaning in all the way. Our lips touched softly, his were warm and gentle. I felt electricity building in my stomach and traveling throughout my body. My heart began to beat out of my chest. I softly rested my hand on his shoulder, welcoming his embrace. He responded by lightly placing his hand on my waist. I felt like I was floating on a cloud. He pulled back just as slowly and smiled.

"I'll see you tomorrow," he winked.

I nodded back with shaky breath. I turned to open the car door and climbed out with my bookbag. I fumbled to find my keys, dropping them to the pavement. I bent down quickly in embarrassment, unlocking my car and climbing inside. I started the engine and pulled out of the parking lot, heading for home. I was barely able to focus on driving. *I can't believe that just happened,* I thought, *that was amazing.*

I pulled into the driveway and hurried inside the house. My mom was sitting at her pottery wheel, working on a new sculpture. Her hair was pulled back into a messy ponytail with little ringlets framing her face. She had her beige apron on to protect her favorite teal cardigan that she'd gotten from a flea market last summer.

"So, want to tell me where you've been?" She asked. Never looking up from her artwork.

"Um, well, I, uh," I stuttered. "I may have thrown a tantrum and ditched school," I admitted.

"No kidding," she mocked. "Are you going to tell me what happened?"

"Well, you know me, mom, I can never play nice with the other kids," I joked sarcastically.

"Honey, this has got to stop. I know you're angry that we had to move again, but traveling to meet with different dealers is how we make our living. You know that," she scolded, finally looking me in the eye.

"I know, but I just hate always being the new girl, always being judged, never fitting in. High school sucks, and I hate never having any friends!" I exclaimed.

"I know," she replied softly. "I know you do. But it's only for two more months. You'll graduate and be done with it. You can do this; I know you can," she nurtured, standing up from her pottery wheel and walking toward me. She wrapped her arms around me, pulling me in for a hug. I hugged her back, letting out a deep sigh.

"Yeah, I guess you're right," I confessed. "I should probably go do my homework." She nodded back at me in agreement, and I headed for my room.

I closed the door behind me and tossed my backpack onto my bed. I fell back onto it and stared up at the ceiling. I thought about Eric and our afternoon spent together. I replayed the day over and over in my head. A smile instantly spread across my face as my cheeks turned bright red. *Oh God,* I thought, *I can't wait for tomorrow.*

Chapter 2

The next morning, I leaped out of bed with excitement. I completed my morning routine quickly, but made sure to do a little extra makeup today. I grabbed my bookbag and muffin in a hurry and reached for my car keys.

"Somebody's in a hurry today," my mom noted. "I thought you hated school?"

"Yeah, uh, I have to get there early to make up for yesterday. Bye!" I explained and ran out the door.

I pulled into the school's parking lot, scanning the rows for Eric's car. Disappointment filled my chest when I didn't see it. *Maybe he's running late,* I tried to reassure myself.

I spent the day going from class to class, looking for Eric in the hallway but never finding him. I grew more nervous with each passing hour. *Did he come to school today?* I thought. *Is he still going to meet me at the tree stump? What if he doesn't show?*

The end of the day bell rang, and I rushed out of the side door of the school, practically running to the woods. I hurried through the trees and bushes, swatting my way through the woods. I came around the corner to the tree stump and my heart jumped out of my chest. *He came.*

"Hey!" I greeted him a little too eagerly. I cleared my throat in an effort to hide my excitement. Eric sat on the tree stump, looking down at his feet, refusing to meet my gaze.

"Are you okay?" I asked gently.

He paused for a moment before slowly lifting his head. He had a black eye.

"Oh, my God! What happened? Are you okay?" I questioned, taking a step toward him.

"I, uh-" He was very hesitant with his answer. "I got into a fight with my dad," he confessed. He looked away from me, unable to look me in the eye.

"Wait, your dad did this to you?" I asked gently.

He let out a deep sigh, still looking away from me.

"Yeah," he whispered.

"Oh, Eric," I whispered back. My heart sank. I took another slow step toward him. I reached out my hand and gently brushed the side of his face. "I'm so sorry," I choked. I felt the tears wallowing in my eyes. He took my hand, bringing my fingers to his lips, kissing them softly.

"It's okay Luna, I'll be all right," he reassured me.

He stood up onto his feet and pulled me into is chest. I laid my head against his shoulder, wrapping my arms around his back tightly. He buried his face in my neck, letting out a deep exhale. We stood there for a few moments, holding each other in silence. I listened to the sound of his heartbeat, finding it more comforting than a lullaby.

Eric pulled away gently, looking deeply into my eyes. He lifted his hand and brushed my hair behind my ear, with his other hand still wrapped around my waist.

"Why don't you stay at my place tonight?" I offered.

Eric paused for a moment, looking as though I caught him off guard with my suggestion.

"Unless you don't want to," I quickly countered, worried I'd overstepped.

"No, I want to. I really want to." He smiled.

"Okay." I smiled back.

Eric leaned in, pressing his lips against mine, kissing me deeply and passionately. The world faded away as I sunk into him. A spark grew in my gut, building and electrifying throughout my entire body. Who needed shooting stars when being around by him could give me such a rush?

We walked back out of the woods together, heading toward the parking lot, hand in hand, smiling childishly at each other.

We got into our cars, and Eric followed me back to my house. I felt myself smiling like an idiot the whole way home. I was barely able to concentrate on how to drive.

I pulled into my driveway, parking next to my mom's old station wagon while Eric parked on the street. We walked up to the front door together and I let us inside. My mom was back at her pottery wheel, deep in focus on a project.

"Hey, mom," I greeted her.

She jumped up, startled by my voice.

"Oh, hi honey," she replied, still not looking up from her pottery.

"This is a new friend of mine, Eric," I said nervously.

My mom quickly looked up from her work, staring wide eyed at Eric.

"Oh Eric, it's so nice to meet you!" She greeted him. She jumped up from her stool and walked up to Eric with open arms. She was very short compared to him but gave him, but she gave him a welcoming hug regardless.

Eric hugged her back awkwardly, seeming unfamiliar with the introduction to a parent. "Hey, it's nice to meet you. I hope it's okay that I'm here." He hesitated.

"Oh of course sweetie! The more the merrier," my mom comforted. "Oh, honey that doesn't look very good," she added, pointing at Eric's black eye.

"Mom!" I yelled, giving her a look of embarrassment.

"Why don't I get you some ice for that?" she said to Eric, ignoring me.

"Oh, uh, that'd be great, thanks." Eric replied embarrassed.

My mom turned away toward the kitchen and I turned to Eric mouthing the words, "I'm sorry," to him. He waved his hand that it wasn't a big deal, but I felt the uncomfortableness growing.

My mom handed him an ice pack and we headed back to my room. I opened the door, immediately realizing how messy my room was. Unpacked boxes cluttered the floor around my unmade bed.

"I'm sorry for the mess," I blurted out.

Eric walked in behind me, taking in the room, observing the space.

"I don't mind," he reassured me. "Looks like you have some unpacking to do," he teased.

I looked away, feeling my cheeks flush.

"Yeah, most of it is my art supplies and work. I just haven't gotten to it yet," I admitted.

Intrigued, Eric bent down and opened one of the boxes. I half step forward, hesitant on what might be inside. He pulled out my folded-up easel. He stepped over to the corner on the other end of the room, unfolding the structure and setting it up into place.

"You paint?" he asked, turning back to the box.

"A little," I replied sheepishly as he pulled out brushes and a painter's tray. He sets the supplies down on a small table next to the easel.

"Let me see your work." He requests.

"Oh, it's not that good." I mutter, playing with the sleeves on my shirt.

"Oh, come on, Picasso. Let me see," he teased.

I smiled back at him sheepishly. "Okay." I hesitated. I walked over to a large, black zip around case that was leaning against the wall. I unzipped it and carefully pull out a large canvas. I carried it over to the easel gently placing a painting on it. I took a step back, looking to Eric, examining his expression. He took a step forward, observing the painting closely. It was my most recent work of art, a detailed portrait of my mother, sitting at her pottery wheel with her beige apron, looking deep in thought as she sculpted her clay. It was my best work and also my most personal one. Eric stood silent for several moments taking in every brush stroke.

"This, is amazing," he exhaled. He turned toward me; his face lit up in amazement. "Luna, you're so talented. This should be in a museum!" he exclaimed.

My cheeks turned red, and a smile escaped my lips.

"Oh, thank you," I replied. "My dream is to go to Rhode Island's School of Design. It's the best art school in the country."

"Have you applied?" he questioned.

"Of course," I mocked. "But it's a very competitive school, the chances of me going there are little to none," I admitted, looking down at my feet.

"Hey, have some faith in yourself. You're very talented, I think you have a very high chance of going." He smiled.

I smiled back at him in appreciation.

I settled into my bed and started on my homework. Eric sat in a white, fluffy chair I had against the wall, scrolling through his phone. I put on some alternative music quietly to fill the air between us.

I glanced over at him frequently, unable to focus on my history paper. His dark grey T-shirt hugged his biceps perfectly, matching the sneakers he wore. A knotted black bracelet lay along his wrist. I'd never noticed it before. *He's so handsome,* I thought.

My mom ordered Chinese for dinner, we sat at the kitchen counter together making small talk as we ate.

"So, Eric, are you from here?" My mom questioned him.

"Yes, I am," he answered.

"What do your parents do?" she asked.

"Mom, please don't interrogate him," I pleaded.

"What?" She asked innocently. "I'm just trying to get to know your new friend," she explained.

"That's okay." Eric defended my mom. "My dad is a welder," he responded.

"And what about your mom?" she asked.

I gave my mom a look to try to get her to stop questioning him.

"Oh, uh, my mom died when I was seven," he replied quietly.

"Oh, honey, I'm so sorry," my mom apologized.

I immediately felt guilty for his confession.

"Oh, that's okay," He comforted her. "I don't mind."

We finished the rest of our meal mostly in silence. My mom blew up an air mattress for Eric to sleep on with some extra blankets we had. She cleared up some space for him on the living room floor, alongside her art supplies. We said our goodnights and my mom, and I headed to our rooms.

I changed into my pajamas and crawled into bed, cocooning myself in my blankets. I scrolled through my phone for a few moments before turning out the light. I rolled over onto my side, trying to get myself comfortable when there was a soft knock on my door. I lifted my head as the door opened softly.

It was Eric. He stepped inside my room, quietly closing the door behind him.

"What are you doing in here?" I whispered, sitting up in my bed.

"I don't want to sleep alone tonight," he whispered back. The pale moonlight shone against his melancholy face. I hesitated for a moment before pulling back the covers as an invitation. Eric climbed into the other side of the bed, wrapping the covers around himself. We both rolled onto our sides, facing each other. I pulled the blankets up to my shoulder and rested my arm between us.

Eric reached out his hand, brushing my hair gently behind my ear. We gazed into each other's eyes, communicating without words. He leaned in, kissing me softly, and wrapped his arms around me, pulling me in close. He kissed me on the forehead, softly stroking his thumb along the middle of my back. I nuzzled my head into his chest and closed my eyes. Listening to the soft beating of his heart, drifting me off to sleep like a lullaby.

Chapter 3

I awoke the next morning to the sound of my alarm. I turned it off and reached out for Eric, but my hand only felt an empty space. I opened my eyes and lifted my head to find that he was gone. There was a folded piece of notebook paper placed on the pillow he'd used:

"Luna,

I didn't want to wake you, you looked so peaceful. Meet me at the tree stump after school.

Eric"

I stared at the note, rereading it over and over again as a smile escaped my lips. I lay back down, holding the note to my chest. Turning to look at the side of the bed where he slept, slowly brushing my hand across the sheets. *Last night was amazing,* I thought to myself, *I can't believe it happened.*

I got myself out of bed and completed my morning routine, heading for the kitchen. My mom was already up making coffee, humming to herself.

"Good morning," she greeted me.

"Good morning," I yawned, taking a large gulp of my coffee.

"Where'd Eric run off to this morning? He was gone when I got up," she questioned.

"I assume he went back home to get ready for school," I explained.

"Okay," she replied. "Did you sleep okay?" she asked suspiciously. I felt the heat rising in my cheeks.

"Oh, yeah, I slept like a log." I hesitated.

"Mmhmm," she mocked, taking a sip of her coffee.

"Oh, boy, look at the time! Don't want to be late for school!" I announced, snatching my keys and rushing toward the front door.

"Have a good day!" my mom called after me. I headed for school, feeling my excitement grow the closer I got there. What a new sensation.

I pulled into the parking lot, scanning the rows again for Eric's car but I couldn't find it. *Is he ditching again?* I thought. *How is he going to graduate if he never goes to class?* I wondered. I headed inside and spent the day learning useless information in each of my classes. Graduation could not come soon enough. I daydreamed about the Rhode Island School of Design. I'd submitted my application back in November, but I still hadn't heard any response. *Where will I go if I don't get in?* I thought. *There's nowhere else that compares to that college, how could I possibly be happy anywhere else?*

The end of the day bell rang, jolting me out of my head. I gathered my things eagerly and heading outside to the woods, walking quickly through the trees. I came around the corner and found Eric sitting on the tree stump. A smile instantly spread across my face as my heart began to raced.

"Hey!" I giggled. He smiled back at me, standing up and walking toward me with his arms open. I welcomed his embrace and hugged him back tightly.

"Why didn't you come to school today?" I asked. "You're never going to graduate if you keep ditching you know."

"Yeah, I know." He smirked. "But you know school isn't really my thing. Especially not this place."

"I know but how are you going to pursue your dream of living in Colorado if you don't have a diploma?" I countered.

"Well, there are plenty of jobs out there I can do that don't require me to graduate. Plus, I could start at the bottom somewhere and work my way up. Sure, it'll take some time, but I'm not in any rush. Besides, I already have a plan," he explained. Eric took a step back toward the tree stump, looking down at large duffle bag leaning against it.

He looked back up toward me with a sympathetic look in his eyes. My heart sank into my gut, and I could feel a golf-ball sized lump growing in my throat. I took a step back, not wanting to acknowledge the truth.

"Eric," I whimpered. "You're not leaving now, are you?"

He took a step toward me. Reaching out to hold my hands, he interlaced his fingers in mine, looking deep into my eyes.

"Luna, I can't stay here anymore. I can't live another day in my father's house, I can't waste another second in that stupid school, I don't belong here," he replies.

I felt my breath catch in my throat; my eyes begin to welled up.

"Come with me," he pleaded.

"What?" I whispered.

"Come with me, Luna. Come with me to Colorado. We could live in the mountains together. You can paint and I can build us a home, and it'll just be the two of us, forever," he persuaded.

I took a step back from him, letting go off his hands. "Eric, I can't," I cried. "My mom is here, I want to go to college in Rhode Island, I want to be a successful artist. I have to graduate in order to do those things. I can't just leave."

"Yes, you can. You can still do all those things. Just do them in Colorado with me!" He cried.

Tears fell down my cheeks, I could feel my lips trembling. "Please, you can't leave me. Just wait a little longer-just stay here with me. You can live at my house, we can graduate, you can come with me to college. We can live together there and be happy. Please Eric, don't leave me," I pleaded.

"Luna," he exhaled, reaching out to me, placing his hands on my shoulders. "That's not my dream. I can't get into college, I don't want to live in some city that I don't belong, I mean, what would I even do there?"

"Be with me?" I explained. Eric reached out his hand, wiping the tears from my cheek.

"Luna," he whispered, "I want to be with you, more than anything. But I don't belong in Rhode Island."

I dropped my head, looking down at the ground. Tears blurred my vision. Eric leaned forward, kissing the top of my head gently.

"I'm sorry," he said softly. "But I have to go." He placed his finger under my chin, lifting my head gently, meeting my gaze. "I'll come find you. Once I make something of myself, I promise, I will come find you. This isn't the end for us," he comforted me.

"Eric," I sobbed.

"I know." He whispered. He leaned in, pressing his lips against mine. I wrapped my arms around his neck as he wrapped his around my back. It was passionate, dreamlike, gentle. Eric pulled away slowly; I didn't want to let go. He reached up, lifting my hands from his shoulders, bringing one hand to his lips, kissing my fingers softly. He dropped my hands gently before turning to reach down and grab his duffle. He threw the bag over his shoulder and began to walk away.

He took several steps before stopping, pausing for a moment and turning to look back at me. His gaze meets mine, tortured and in pain. Then he turned back and walked out of the woods, gone from my line of sight.

I dropped to my knees. Covering my eyes with both of my hands, uncontrollable sobs escaping me. I couldn't contain this pain I felt inside. I lowered a hand to my chest, and covered my heart, I felt it breaking. Shattering. *How could he leave me?* I thought. *How could he just walk away? When will I see him again?* Endless thoughts swirled my head as the tears poured down my face.

I remained kneeling for several moments before I took a deep, shaky breath as I tried to wipe my face dry. I sniffled and calmed myself back down. I took a moment before I stood back up on my feet. I felt wobbly, unstable, cold. I wrapped my arms around myself and slowly put one foot in front of the other, making my way out of the woods.

The parking lot was empty, all of the other students had already gone home. I envied them for not losing someone they love.

I drove home in silence, no music, no words, no thoughts. Silence.

I parked my car in the driveway, grabbing my bookbag and heading for the door, dreading my mother's interrogation.

I slipped inside the front door, finding her sitting at her pottery wheel. I walked past her quickly, avoiding eye contact, trying to hide my face. Racing straight for my room, I closed the bedroom door behind me and collapsed into my bed. I pulled my blankets over my head and buried my face in my pillow, shutting out the world.

I let out an exhale, feeling a small sense of relief when I smell his cologne. I pull the pillow he slept on to my nose and inhale deeply. *Eric,* I thought. I can't escape the pain, even in my safe place, cocooned in my blankets. Even here, he lingered. I reached out my hand to the side where he'd slept, and I felt my eyes begin to water again. I buried my face into my pillow, letting out soft sobs when there was a knock at the door. I immediately wiped my face, trying to hide my sorrow.

"Honey?" my mom called, slowly opening my bedroom door.

"Yeah?" I answered, still buried under the blankets.

"Are you okay?" she asked gently.

"Yea," I choked out. "I just don't feel good."

"Okay." she replies, sitting down on the end of my bed. I can feel her place her hand on my leg. "I have something that might help."

"I'm not really in the mood for one of your special teas, mom." I exhaled.

"It's not tea, sweetie, although I'm happy to make you some," she offered.

"No thanks." I mumbled.

"Come on," she urged, pulling at my blankets. "This will cure anything."

"Mom," I groaned and pulled back at the blankets.

"Oh, would you just come out of there!" She exclaimed, tossing something at me.

I groaned and pulled the blankets down off my head, brushing the hair out of my face. "What?" I grouched. She gestures toward a large white envelope that lay in the bed. I roll my eyes and pick it up, looking at the cover. It's from the Rhode Island School of Design. My eyes grew wide as I looked back at my mom. She raised her eyebrows and smirked mockingly.

"Well, open it!" She yelled. I let out a deep breath and tear open the envelope, pulling out a large packet with a cover letter. I grab the letter eagerly and begin to read:

Dear Miss Hart,

We are pleased to inform you that you have been accepted to the Rhode Island School of Design.

I jumped up out of bed, screaming. My mom jumped up in unison and hugged me tightly. She spun me around in a circle as we cheer and dance in celebration.

"Congratulations!" She applauded, "Oh honey, I'm so proud of you!"

"Thanks mom." I smiled.

My hands shook as I look back down at the letter, filled with disbelief, excitement and nerves. *I can't believe I did it,* I thought. A smile filled my face as I reread it over and over.

"This calls for red velvet cake!" She clapped. "I'll run to the store and get some!"

My mom ran out the room and I sat back down on my bed.

I can't believe I did it.

Chapter 4

I woke up to the ringing of my alarm. I jolted up right in bed, excited for what the day is going to bring. Hopping onto my feet, I headed for the shower. I blew out my clean hair smoothly and decided to get out my curling iron. I styed loose, beach waves throughout my cherry red hair and painted on a bit more makeup than usual.

I headed back to my room where a white, lace dress with black trim was hanging on my closet door. Slipping it on, I paired it with some white wedged shoes. *Today is the big day,* I thought, *I'm finally graduating.*

I walked out to the kitchen to greet my mom with coffee. She wore her curly hair down and had on a beige sundress. She always decorated her outfits with several pieces of jewelry, layering on various necklaces and bracelets to make her hippie-like aesthetic.

"Good morning, my little graduate!" she cheered.

"Good morning, mom." I smiled.

"Are you ready for the big day?" she questioned.

"You have no idea." I admitted.

We drank our coffee, making small talk before it was time to leave. I grabbed my banana yellow graduation gown and matching cap, running the tassel through my fingers. This doesn't feel real.

My mom and I climbed into her old station wagon and headed for the high school. The sun was shining, and it was a perfect seventy-two-degree day. You couldn't ask for a better setting for an outdoor event. Gazing out the passenger side window, I took in the passing scenery. I let out a deep sigh. Today was the day my life truly began.

We pulled into the crowded parking lot and found a spot, locked our car behind us and made our way toward the football stadium. A sea of yellow and purple graduation gowns filled the football field as my classmates attempted to find their assigned seats. My mom gave me a kiss on the cheek as we parted ways. She headed up the stadium bleachers in search of a seat amongst the other parents.

I let out a deep breath and begin to navigated through the masses. I found my seat on the right side of a large section of chairs. I squeezed down a row of seats until I found one with my name on it. There was a graduation program that was placed on it, I picked it up and took my seat.

The other students settled in as the principal walked up to the podium on a small stage.

"Welcome class of 2024!" he shouted. Everyone clapped in acknowledgement.

He trailed on with a speech about the school's finest achievements. I rolled my eyes and blocked him out. I glanced over at the students sitting on either side of me. I didn't recognize either of them. *I really did ignore all the people here,* I thought to myself. *Oh well, it's not like I'm going to see them again after today anyway. I don't plan on coming back for a reunion in ten years.*

The principal ended his speech and began to announce student's names to come up to the stage to receive their diploma. The first fifty students go up before it was my turn. I followed the row of people in front of me, to line up by the stage.

"Luna Joy Hart," the principal announced, and a quiet applause filtered through the crowd. I took a deep breath. My hands shook. I walked up the side steps and onto the stage. The vice principal handed me my diploma that was wrapped in a perfect scroll with a purple ribbon tied around it. Then, I turned to the principal who shook my hand and gave me a cheesy congratulations. I nodded back in acknowledgment and stepped across the second half of the stage, down the other side of stairs and back down to my seat.

The rest of the class received their diplomas, and the marching band rang out in the graduation song. The students threw their caps in the air and cried out in celebration. I clapped my hands, and a large smile filled my face. I looked down at the diploma in my hand, *I did it,* I thought. *I finally did it. I just graduated high school!*

The celebratory cheering quieted down, and the crowds dispersed. I searched for my mom through the sea of families smiling and hugging. I finally spotted her where the football field meets the bleachers.

"Oh, honey! Congratulations!" she cried out. "I'm so proud of you!" She wrapped her arms around me and pulled me into a tight embrace. I hugged her back lovingly and smiled widely.

"I can't believe it's over." I admitted. "High school is finally over. I did it!"

"You sure did." She smiled; she brushed her finger across my cheek. "What do you say we go out for lunch to celebrate?"

"That's okay mom," I reassured her. "We need to save our money for college."

"Oh, honey don't worry about that. You just graduated high school! Let's go for lunch! You deserve it," she explains.

"Thanks, mom, but how about we settle for some red velvet cake?" I smile. She returned a wide-eyed grin.

"You know I can't resist red velvet cake!" She clapped. We linked arm and arm and headed back to the parking lot to drive home.

We arrived home with cake in hand. I removed my cap and gown carefully, laying them on a kitchen stool. My mom placed the cake on the counter, and we both pulled up a chair. She grabbed two forks out of the drawer, handing me one. We clink forks and dove in, taking large bites out of the cake. We giggled at each other with icing on our faces. My mom wiped a glob of icing onto her finger and wiped it on the tip of my nose, laughing.

"My little graduate." she giggled. I smiled back and wiped the icing from my nose. We enjoyed some more cake before settling in for the rest of the afternoon.

I headed back to my room to change into some sweats before I sat on my stool in front of my art easel. I stretch out my arms before reaching for a paint brush. Staring at a blank canvas, I was unsure of what to paint. I let out a deep sigh before dipping into the paint and giving my brush control. I painted into the evening, not realizing how late it was until my mom called me to come out for dinner. I stood from my stool, giving my neck a good stretch and took a step back to judge my painting. It was a portrait of Eric. I hadn't realize I was even painting him at first. My heart sank, my breath caught in my throat. *Oh Eric,* I thought. *I wish I could've seen him at graduation today. But at least I won't have to go there anymore and have that school as a constant reminder of his presence.*

My mom and I had Italian for takeout, splurging on pasta and breadsticks. She's added three new sculptures to the living room. One of them is almost to the ceiling while the other two are smaller sizes. Her talent never ceased to amaze me.

I stayed up painting for a few more hours before I finally dove into bed. I grabbed my phone and decided to scroll through social media before I turned out the light. I scrolled through Instagram when a post from Eric popped up. My heart dropped. I jolted up in quickly, staring at my phone. It was a photo of the Colorado River at sunset, with the gorges wrapped around it in perfect view.

"*I could get used to this,*" he'd written the caption. I let out a deep sigh and lay back down on my pillow. *At least he's happy,* I thought. I glanced over at the portrait I had painted on my easel for a moment, before I turned out the light.

I spent the next few days packing in preparation for college orientation. I bought a train ticket from Poughkeepsie, New York to Providence, Rhode Island. It was a quick six hours in coach. I packed a few books to read along the way plus my headphones and headache meds, in case I got stuck sitting next to a talker. I also spent my down time working on my painting of Eric some more, feeling both sadness and closure the more in depth it became.

On the morning of my trip, my mom drove me to the train station. I had my backpack and duffle packed to last me through the long weekend. We pulled up to the front curb and my mom put the car in park.

"Well, I wish you safe travels. I know it's going to be overwhelming and chaotic but try to have a little fun while you're there," she reassured me. "And you know you can always call me if you need me."

"Thanks, mom." I replied. I got out of the car, threw my backpack over my shoulder and grabbed my duffle bag. I waved goodbye to my mom and headed inside the train station. It was crowded and loud with people rushing in every direction. I didn't expect it to be so busy at dawn. I walked past several gates before finding the one for my trip. I sat down in an open seat and gazed at the strangers sitting near me. *I need coffee,* I thought to myself. I got up and walked over to a nearby coffee shop and got myself a to-go drink.

    Not too long after, the train arrived at the station for us to board. Since I had a coach ticket, I had to board with the last group but to my surprise there were several empty seats. I took a seat by the window, placing my bags in the chair next to me, hoping no one would ask for it. Luckily, I ended up having the row to myself. The train took off from the station and headed toward Rhode Island. I put in my headphones, playing some alternative music as I pulled out a book to read. It was a novel on different works of art from every country. I sipped on my coffee as the world passed by, excited for orientation.

    A few hours later, we arrived in Providence. I could feel my heart begin pounding in my chest. I eagerly got off the train and headed out to the front curb to call a cab. The warm summer air blasted my cheeks, igniting the excitement within me, as I stepped onto the sidewalk. It was a short drive to the two-story motel I planned to stay at, just by the river. The curb appeal was very run down and unenticing. The cab dropped me off and I checked into a single room. I received one on the second floor which was nice because I wouldn't have to worry about an upstairs neighbor keeping me up at night. I tossed my bags on the bed, glancing around at the hotel room. Dim light reflected against deep maroon walls and brown carpeting. It was nothing special, clean but cheap.

I decided to order some takeout for dinner and analyze the orientation packet I had received, in anticipation for tomorrow. An old square television quietly played cartoons, but I drowned out the white noise, daydreaming of the following day. I went to bed early that night, eager to start the next day.

I awoke in the following morning to the sun shining in through the beige curtains. I hopped in the shower and got myself ready to face the day. It was overcast with a light breeze, but the day still carried the heat of summer. After grabbing a quick cup of coffee, I called another cab to take me to campus.

It was beautiful. More beautiful than any picture I had seen on the school's website. The red brick buildings lining the street, the coffee carts, the large art sculptures, everything on campus was beautiful. I felt my heart skip a beat in my chest. My cab dropped me off right out front of the design building. I climbed out of the car and froze, staring up at the building before me in awe. *I actually get to go here,* I thought. Pinching my arm, I needed to make sure I wasn't dreaming.

I followed the orientation signs to the resource fair. I walked along several different tables, listening to different students and staff give their speeches. I received several flyers and endless information. I took a moment of pause, listening to the leaves dance in the wind, allowing myself to truly inhale this moment.

After the resource fair, I spent the rest of the afternoon learning about residence life, financial aid and had a meeting with my guidance counselor. By the end of the night, I had a migraine from the overwhelming day. Yet I was filled with more joy than I thought was possible. So, I decided to head back to the hotel for the night and dove straight into bed.

The following day, I took an in-depth tour of campus and discovered where the best coffee carts were located. The library was one of my favorite places to visit-observing the number of art books offered, was astonishing. My feet feltl annoyingly sore, with the endless amount of walking.

As the second day ended, the campus hosted an end-of-orientation carnival. I debated on whether or not I wanted to go, but I ended up talking myself into attending. There were fair games, cotton candy stands, hot dog stands, and of course coffee carts. I walked through the crowds, people watching and observing the families celebrating together. Most of the students were here with their parents. I quickly felt very alone. Trying to find comfort, I walked over to get in line at one of the coffee carts.

"Are you alone here too?" a boy asked. I turned around to a find a tall, built guy with light brown hair that was perfectly cut and styled. His brown eyes were illuminated by the twinkling carnival lights surrounding us.

"Uh, yeah, my mom had to stay back home," I hesitated.

"Same with my folks. They couldn't get the time off," he explained.

"I know the feeling," I replied.

"I'm Collin, by the way," he greeted me, reaching out his hand. I shook his hand back quickly, feeling very awkward.

"I'm Luna," I responded. It was finally my turn to order. I grabbed my coffee and awkwardly turn back to Collin. "Well, uh, it was nice meeting you." I hesitated.

"Yeah, maybe I'll see you around campus sometime." he smiled. I nodded back and turned to walk away. I don't know why making new friends always had to be so uncomfortable for me.

I headed back to the train station the next morning, making my way back home. My mom picked me up from the train station, drilling me with about a hundred questions. To quiet her down, I gave her a shirt I bought from the gift shop. She squealed with joy, eager to try it on.

When we arrived back home and settled in, I realized I needed to hunt for a summer job. I'd been paying my way for a while now, but college was going to be different. I headed to bed for the night, scrolling on my phone before turning out the light when I saw an ad for a barista at Starbucks. *I guess I couldn't find a better job than one that pays me to drink coffee, I thought.*

Chapter 5

Summer passed in a blur. I spent most of my days working at Starbucks, trying to save up as much money as possible. I memorized every recipe in the shop and moved up to three cups of coffee a day. I really need to cut back.

With only two weeks left until move in day, I received an email from the school's residential office, alerting me that I had been matched with a roommate. Her name was Kaitlin, another freshman from Columbus, Ohio. I opened the email finding her contact information and that we would be living in Homer Hall together. I saved her phone number in my contacts and decided to shoot her a text message.

"Hey Kaitlin, it's Luna, your new roommate.

I just got the email that we've been matched to live together.

What time do you plan on moving in?" I hesitated for a moment before pressing send.

I set my phone down and let out a deep exhale. *How was I supposed to share a room with a stranger for the next nine months?* I thought. *What if she's mean? What if she hates me? What if we don't get along? Would I have to move out? What if I can't find another dorm?*

My phone dinged, pulling me out of my thoughts. I wiped my sweaty palms on my shorts and reached for my phone.

"Hey Luna! I'm so glad you reached out!

I just received the email too; I think my parents are planning on us arriving at 8 a.m.

That way we have all day to get settled. What about you?

Have you started buying stuff for our room?" she replied.

I paused, rereading the text message over. *Well, so far she seems nice enough,* I thought. *Oh, God, I didn't even think about planning out our room together. What if she doesn't like the stuff I've already bought?* I took a deep breath before responding.

"I'll try and get there at 8:30, that way you have some time to yourself.

And yeah, I've bought a couple of things, but nothing major yet.

I wasn't sure if you wanted to coordinate anything." I replied.

I'd tried to keep my spending minimal. Only buying the necessities like a shower cady, some pens and notebooks, a desk lamp, and a show rack for my closet.

"No worries! I want you to bring what you're comfortable with.

I did get a black futon for our room; I hope that's ok.

I also got a beige tapestry and some picture frames for the walls.' she replied.

Looks like I'm going to have to do some more shopping, I thought.

I grabbed my black crossbody purse and car keys, heading out the door. I drove straight to the mall and spent the entire afternoon buying decorations for the dorm room as well as some new bedding and small decorative paintings to hang up. *I feel like this is all such a waste of money,* I thought, *but I want to make a good first impression on Kaitlin.*

I arrived back home, just in time for dinner. I carried all of my new purchases to my bedroom where I found some moving boxes and packaging tape.

"Honey! Dinners ready!" my mom called. I headed out to the kitchen where she was unboxing a large pizza. "I hope you're hungry."

"Starved." I replied.

"Did you get a bunch of good stuff today?" she questioned. I nodded in response with a mouth full of food. "I've got some cash I want to give you after we finish eating."

"Oh, mom, you don't have to do that," I consoled her.

"Oh, stop. Let me help you with your spending." she requested.

I shrugged my shoulders, giving in to her offer.

We finished dinner and I headed back to my room. *I guess I better start packing,* I thought.

Over the next two weeks, after work, I spent all my free time packing up each of my belongings until moving day arrived. It was a three-hour drive to the school, so in order to meet Kaitlin on time, my mom and I had to leave the house at five in the morning. A much shorter journey than my train ride from orientation that had several stops along the way. My mom helped me load up the station wagon, overfilling the car with all of my boxes. We drank a cup of coffee together before hitting the road. We both yawned in unison as we climbed into the car, buckling up for the road trip.

We pull out of the driveway and headed toward our destination. My mom turned on the radio to try to keep us awake. The headlights of the car beamed against the dark road. The stars twinkled in the sky, watching over us, filled me with hope. I thought about Eric, how I gazed out at the scenery passing by that day we ditched school together. I leaned my head against the passenger side window, letting out a deep exhale. I could feel an ache in my chest. *God, I miss him,* I thought.

We make our way through Connecticut as the sun began to rise. The orange glow filled us with warmth and energy. I took in a deep breath, eager to get to campus.

"Now, don't forget to always wear flip flops to the shower. Oh, and you might want to buy your own toilet paper, just in case. And always double check you have your keycard before you leave your room," my mom reminded me.

"Okay, okay, mom. I promise to do all of those things," I replied.

"And you know you can always call me, no matter what," she spoke softly, reaching for my hand. "I don't know what I'm going to do without my girl."

I felt a lump growing in my throat.

"I'm going to miss you, too, mom." I admitted, squeezing her hand gently. She spent the last leg of the car ride giving me tips and reminders for what to do at school.

We arrived at the school, at 8:30 exactly. The campus was swarmed with families. Parents and students lugged their items from their cars into their dorms. Cars were parked in the middle of the street, desperately trying to fit through. We squeezed through traffic until we finally made it to my dorm building. My mom was able to pull into a spot, right as another car was leaving. We hopped out and I went inside the front doors of the building. The lobby was packed with people rushing in and out. There was a residential advisor standing in the middle of the room in a neon green shirt. My mom and I approached her to check in. She gave me my room number and directed me to where I could receive my student ID.

We headed back out to the car and immediately grabbed as much as we could carry. My mom followed me back inside the dorm, arms full as we tried to find our way to my room. It was on the first floor, toward the end of the hallway by a side door. I approached the room, finding that the door was already open. I walked in to find a tall, slender blonde with wavy hair that had a pink feather in it. She was hanging up picture frames above a desk on the opposite side of the room. I set my box down on the floor and cleared my throat.

"Hey." I greeted awkwardly. She turned around quickly with a large smile.

"Hey! You must be Luna!" She replied warmly. She stepped toward me and gave me a welcoming hug. "I'm so happy to finally meet you. I hope you don't mind; I took the top bunk." She announced, pointing toward the bunkbeds.

"Oh, no, that's fine," I said coolly. I turned to let my mom in the room behind me. "Oh, and this is my mom."

"Hello sweetie, I'm Sammy," my mom smiled, reaching out her hand to Kaitlin's.

"Hi, it's so nice to meet you!" Kaitlin replied enthusiastically. "Well, let me get out of your way, I'm sure you have a lot to unpack."

I nodded in response, placing my box on the bottom bunkbed. My mom and I finished unpacking the car, carrying everything into my room. We started opening the boxes when a tall, skinny woman with short, straight, blonde hair walked into the room. She wore a navy blazer with matching dress pants. Behind her walked in an even taller man with short, brown hair who wore a striped dress shirt. They both had very stern expressions.

"Oh, mom, dad, I want you to meet my new roommate, Luna." Kaitlin introduced us. My mom and I turned toward them in acknowledgement. I immediately felt self-conscious in my black sweatpants.

"Hello, I'm Luna's mom, Sammy," my mom smiled, reaching out her hand. Kaitlin's mother paused, looking my mom up and down before a fake smile escaped her lips. She reached out to shake my mom's hand slowly, as if afraid to make contact.

"It's lovely to meet you," she snickered.

"Hello," the man spoke coldly.

I let out a shaky breath, feeling the tension rise in the room.

"Are you from Rhode Island?" My mom asked kindly.

"No. We're from Ohio." Kaitlin's mother replied. "We're very proud of our Kaitlin for getting in to such a prestigious school." She spoke unemotionally. Kaitlin half smiled at her mother's cold compliment. "Well, we really must be going," she announced.

"Let me walk you out," Kaitlin offered.

The couple turned to leave, with Kaitlin following quickly behind them. I turned to my mom with a sympathetic expression.

"Well, that was uncomfortable," I stated.

"Yeah, they were very pleasant weren't they?" She replied sarcastically. We both let out a giggle before turning back to unpacking my boxes.

I made my new bed with a violet-colored bedding and hung a few small pieces of artwork along the wall, next to Kaitlin's pictures. A beige, woven tapestry was hung across the main, middle wall. With a black futon that was set up under a large window, perpendicular to the tapestry, I took a step back, taking in the entire room. To my surprise, I liked it. It was comfortable and cute, not too overwhelming. My mom linked her arm with mine and let out a sigh.

"Everything looks great," she smiled.

"It does, doesn't it?" I replied.

"Well, it's about that time," she nudged. "I should probably hit the road."

My heart felt heavy. I didn't anticipate saying goodbye would be so difficult. I was so eager to go to college that I forgot to mourn the separation from my mom.

"I guess so. I'll walk you out to your car," I offered.

Kaitlin was seated at her desk, organizing, and gave a kind wave to my mom as we left the room. We walked arm and arm down the front steps and to the curb where her car waited.

"Well, kid," she spoke, brushing my red hair from my face. "This is where we part ways."

"Yeah, I guess it is," I said sadly.

"Give it sometime. You'll be just fine without me." She winked. A small smile escaped my lips.

"I love you, mom," I said as I wrapped my arms around her, hugging her tightly.

"I love you too, sweetheart," she soothed, hugging me back. I let out a deep sigh and let her go. She climbed into the car and slowly pulled away from the curb, heading back home. I felt an empty pit fill my gut. We'd never been apart before. I already missed her. I placed my hand over my heart and took in a deep breath, before turning to head back into the dorm.

Chapter 6

Once Kaitlin and I were fully settled into our new dorm room, she suggested we go out and meet our neighbors. I followed her out into the hallway, locking the door behind me. There were two cut out pineapples taped to our door, one with my name written across it and the other with Kaitlin's. *How weird,* I thought, *this is my new home.*

Kaitlin knocked on the door of the room directly to the left of ours. We were at the end of the hallway, so we only had to share a wall with one room which was nice.

"Hello." A brunette girl with round glasses greeted us.

"Hi, I'm Kaitlin, and this is my roommate Luna! We live next door and wanted to come over and introduce ourselves." Kaitlin answered cheerfully.

"Oh, hi!" The brunette smiled, "Come on in! My roommate isn't moving in until tomorrow so it's just me for now." She stepped to the side, allowing us to enter her room. It was overwhelming, decorated with bright yellow decorations everywhere.

"Your room is so cute!" Kaitlin complimented her, "Would you like to go get some coffee with Luna and me?"

"Absolutely!" She grabbed her key and walked out of the room behind us.

We knocked on the door of one other room, meeting two other girls who also agreed to join us. Luckily, Kaitlin did all of the talking, allowing me to stay in my shell.

We headed over to the east side transit tunnel to ride over to Bolt Coffee Shop. The small store front was swarming with other freshman. I felt my stomach clench at the overwhelming atmosphere. As an introvert, this was the exact type of situation I usually tried to avoid.

We received our coffees and headed back outside, making our way over to Memorial Park. We found an open space of grass by the Providence River and sat down together. I sipped my coffee listening to the other girls introduce themselves. One of them came from California, an aspiring artist who specialized in pottery. Another girl was a painter like me, but she preferred a nature painting style as opposed to my portrait style. Kaitlin explained that she was a photographer and made her way working weddings. She also enjoyed illustrating and wanted to write her own children's book with her own drawings. As she spoke about her passions, I noticed a butterfly tattoo on her inner forearm. It was delicate but highly detailed. I envied her for having a tattoo. I couldn't wait to receive my first one.

As nerve racking as it was to be socializing with these girls, it was nice to actually make some friends for once. I felt more encouraged about my living situation.

After we finished our coffees, we grabbed dinner before we headed back to our dorms for the evening. I settled in at my desk, going over my class schedule for the week and the syllabi for each lecture.

"Are you nervous about to starting classes tomorrow?" Kaitlin questioned. I looked up from my desk and turned toward her.

"Ver,." I admitted. I picked at a hole in my ripped jeans, unable to make eye contact.

"Me, too," she replied. "My stomach is a wreck just thinking about it." I was relieved to

hear her honestly. *Maybe I don't have to be so guarded around her,* I thought.

"Uh, today was nice. Meeting our neighbors." I spoke weakly.

"Yeah, it was nice, wasn't it? We should have them over for a movie night sometime," she suggested. "Unless that's too much for you. I noticed you were a bit on the quiet side today, and I don't want to overstep."

I felt the heat rising in my cheeks, and my breathing turned shallow.

"Uh, no." I hesitated. "That sounds great. Maybe we could have them over this weekend."

God why am I so awkward? I thought.

We changed into our pajamas and settled into our bunkbeds. I set an alarm on my phone and set it down on my desk right next to me.

"Goodnight," I spoke as I turned out the light.

"Goodnight!" Kaitlin replied kindly. I pulled the blankets up to my chin, turning on to my side, trying to get comfortable when my phone dinged. I frowned as I reached to grab it, and it was a text message from Eric. My heart sank.

"Come outside," he wrote. I tilted my head in confusion. *Come outside?* I thought. *Is he outside of my house back in New York? There's no way he could be here.*

"I'm not at home anymore. I'm in Rhode Island at school," I replied. A text bubble popped up, I felt my heart race.

"I know. Come outside," he responded. *There's no way,* I thought. I climbed out of bed quietly, sliding on my slippers and black robe. I grabbed my key and slowly slipped out the door, locking it behind me. I raced down the hall, heading out to the main lobby. My heart was pounding in my chest, butterflies stirred in my stomach. I reached for the front door and yanked it open without hesitation. I stepped out onto the front stoop panting, and there he was. In his black jeans and matching black T-shirt, the same outfit he'd worn when I met him. He held a bouquet of liles in one hand.

"I wanted to come surprise you. I hope that's okay." He hesitated. I took in a deep breath before I ran down the front steps, onto the sidewalk and jumping into his arms. I wrapped my hands around his neck as he wrapped his arms around my waist, lifting me up into the air and twirling me around in a circle. Laughter escaped my lips as her spun me. He slowly lowered me back to the ground, never letting go. I looked up into his bright blue eyes, shining back at me. I lunged forward, pressing my lips against his.

He kissed me back deeply, with a longing that words couldn't express. He lifted his hand to my cheek, brushing it gently back through my hair, resting it on my neck. I felt my eyes watering. I'd never felt joy like I felt in this moment. I pulled my lips back from him softly, never letting go of each other.

"I can't believe you're here," I whispered. A wide smile spreads across his cheeks.

"Surprise," he chuckled. "I had to see you. You have no idea how much I've missed you these past few months."

"Oh, I think I have a very good idea." I laughed. He leaned in and kissed me again before pulling me into his embrace. I rested my head on his shoulder, nuzzling into his neck. I inhaled his cologne. It smelled like home. He brushed his hand along the middle of my back, resting his head against mine. We stood there for a moment, taking in each other's presence.

"Can you stay the night?" I whispered.

"Just try to stop me," he chuckled. I pulled back from him, unable to contain my smile. I took the flowers, lifting them to my nose and smelling their aroma. Pure joy. I reached for his hand and pulled him toward the building, he walked beside me up the front steps and inside. He followed me down the hall to my room.

Before unlocking the door, I turned to him, lifting my finger to lips, gesturing him to be quiet. He nodded in acknowledgement and followed me inside the room. It was pitch dark. I reached my hand out to guide us toward the bunk bed, Eric slipped off his shoes and climbed into the bottom bunk. He turned onto his side facing me, with his back up against the wall.

I kicked off my slippers and tossed my robe on to the futon, climbing into bed next to him. We pulled the blankets up to our shoulders, cuddling in close. He pulled me into his embrace. I wrapped my arm around his back, nuzzling my face into his chest as he rested his head on top of mine.

"Goodnight, my Luna," he whispered. A smile filled my face.

"Goodnight, my Eric," I whispered back. I listened to the sound of his heartbeat as he brushed his hand up and down the middle of my back. The beating was smoother than a lullaby, comforting me to sleep.

I awoke the next morning to my alarm ringing in my ears. I grumbled as I rolled away from Eric to silence my phone. I rubbed my eyes, squinting against the stream of sunlight shining in through the curtains. I rolled back over into Eric's arms. He let out a sleepy sigh and kissed me on the forehead.

"Good morning!" Kaitlin called out. My eyes shot open as the top bunk shook to her climbing down.

"Oh, uh, good morning." I hesitated, quickly shuffling onto my feet. Kaitlin hopped down on to the ground and took one look at me. Her eyes grew wide as she spotted Eric stretched out in my bed. She glanced back at him then back at me, her jaw dropping to the floor. She tugged at her top, attempting to straighten it out and brushing her hair out of her face.

"Uh, good morning," she hesitated, standing very awkwardly.

"This is my, uh, this is Eric," I introduced sheepishly. "He surprised me last night after we had gone to bed. I hope you don't mind that he spent the night."

"Oh, no, it's fine," she tried to accommodate us. "Well, I'd better get in the shower." She grabbed her supplies and headed out to the bathroom. She closed the door behind her, and I turned to Eric. We both busted out laughing.

"Well, I guess we better get ready too," I suggested, trying to contain my laughter. "There's a coffee shop over on the other side of campus that I'd like to take you to."

"Sounds great," Eric replied, stretching his arms. We both got up for the day and got ourselves ready. I asked Kaitlin if she wanted to join us, but she politely declined, saying she wanted to get to class early.

Eric and I exited the dorm and headed to the transit tunnel to ride over to the Bolt Coffee Shop.

We entered the coffee shop; it was busy but not as overwhelming as it had been the day before. We ordered our coffees and a few danishes before finding a booth in the back corner. It was comfortable, a cotton seat with a wooden table. The walls were painted a dark green with plants hanging from the ceiling. It was a very calming atmosphere.

"So, how's Colorado?" I asked Eric as I took a sip from my red coffee mug.

"It's pretty good so far. I found a job as a delivery truck driver for FedEx. It's nothing special but it's made me enough cash to buy an old RV off this guy I work with. I've fixed it up and found an acre to live on. It's actually pretty nice. It's quiet and peaceful, but it also gets kind of lonely." He paused, looking down at his danish. "Maybe you can come out and visit me sometime soon?" He asked hesitantly. I reached out and grabbed his hand.

"I would love to." I smiled. "Maybe over winter break."

"I'd love that." He smiled back. "I've also decided to get my GED. If I want to make anything of myself, I'm going to need my degree. I wish I had finished high school like you had suggested but I also had to get out of there."

"I know you did. I don't blame you for leaving as early as you did," I comforted him. My heart began to ache at the memory of him leaving and the thought of him leaving me again. "How long are you able to stay?"

"Well, I actually need to leave after this," He hesitated. "I only got two days off work and I'm going to need to get on the road soon to make it back in time." My heart sank.

"Oh," I replied, slowly pulling my hand back to my coffee cup. "I wish we had more time."

"I know. I do, too," he reassured me. "But we'll be able to see each other again soon."

"Yeah, I guess so," I whispered. We finished our breakfast and headed out of the coffee shop. I walked with Eric across campus to where his car was parked. We walked hand in hand, people watching and observing different buildings and statues as we walked.

We arrived at his car, parked in a lot by my dorm building. He turned, leaning his back up against the car, pulling my hands up and placing them around his neck. He wrapped his arms around my back, holding me close. He smiled down at me, brushing my hair away from my face. I felt my eyes begin to well up.

"Hey," he said, brushing my cheek. "There's no need for tears."

"I'm sorry." I whispered. "I just hate that you're leaving me again." He dropped his head, looking away from my gaze.

"I know," he choked. "I hate that I have to leave you. I want so desperately for you to come back with me, but I know it's selfish of me to ask that of you." He lifted his head, meeting my gaze slowly. Tears welled up in his eyes. I felt mine begin to run down my cheeks, trying desperately to choke back by sobs.

"Please don't leave me." I cried. Eric leaned forward and kissed me on the forehead, holding me for a moment before pulling away from me and turning to get into his car. I took a step back and watched as he started the car and buckled himself in. He turned to look back at me through the window and mouthed 'I love you' as a tear escaped and ran down his cheek. His car slowly pulled away from the curb, driving away from me, once again.

Chapter 7

The first week of classes passed by in a blur. By the end of the week, I was finally feeling used to sitting in giant lecture halls with professors who were way more relaxed than any high school teacher I'd ever had. Since it was syllabus week, I luckily didn't have any homework yet, so I spent most of my time at the coffee shop. I always sat in the booth in which Eric, and I had breakfast, or I roamed campus for quiet benches to sit on and people watch.

I came home from my last class on Friday. It was around dinner time, and my stomach was eager to remind me that it was chicken nugget day at the dining hall.

"Hey!" Kaitlin greeted me as I walked into our dorm room.

"Hey, what's up?" I replied, hanging my bookbag onto the back of my desk chair.

"I was just getting ready to grab some dinner. Do you want to come with me?" she asked as she touched up her makeup.

"Sure, I'm starving," I agreed, slumping down onto the futon.

"Great! Oh, and since it's finally the weekend, I was thinking about going out to some of the parties that Greek life is throwing. It's rush week so all of the fraternities and sororities will be throwing huge ragers." She exclaimed.

"Oh, I don't know." I sighed, pulling at my shirt.

"Oh, come on, Luna. You've got to get out of this room. You're coming with me even if I have to drag you there myself," she smirked.

"Ugh, fine," I grunted, rolling my eyes.

We grabbed our key cards and headed out for the dining hall. There was a massive line outside the building, but luckily, they moved pretty quickly. We got inside and I headed straight for the chicken nuggets and French fries. *So freaking good,* I thought.

I met Kaitlin at a table against the back wall that was lined with windows. We sat down and immediately dug into our food.

"So, what does your mom do?" Kaitlin asked between mouthfuls.

"She's a freelance artist. We travel across the country in search of buyers, but her real dream is to one day open her own art studio." I explained.

"That's so cool! Way more interesting than my parents. I can see where you get your creative genes," she teased.

"Yeah, I guess so. Except moving around all of the time gets really old really fast." I admitted. "What do your parents do?"

"My parents own Butterfly Inn," she admitted cautiously. I choked on a fry at her confession.

"Your parents own Butterfly Inn?" I gasped. "That's like the biggest lodging company in the world!"

"Yeah," she said sheepishly. "I don't like to tell many people because then everyone wants to befriend me for the money and fame."

"Oh, I'm sorry. People suck." I spoke, giving her a sympathetic smile.

"You're telling me." She smiled back, and we both laughed as we finished eating our dinner.

When we got back to the dorm, Kaitlin took over as my makeover guide. She flung open my tiny closet doors and got to work. She flipped through each of my clothing items before she turned toward me with a judgmental glare.

"Dude, everything in this closet is either ripped jeans or plain B-shirts in either black, maroon or violet."

"What can I say, I know what I like." I gave her my best sarcastic smile.

"Next weekend, we're going shopping," she replied, rolling her eyes at me. "All right, looks like I'm lending you one of my things."

"Oh God, nothing too extravagant, please." I hesitated. She turned back toward me, giving me a devilish smirk, before going back through her closet.

"Huh!" She gasped loudly. "This is perfect!" She pulled out a short, black dress with gold, chain straps from her closet.

"Hell, no," I scolded.

"Oh, come on! It's perfect for you! Will you at least humor me and try it on?" she begged.

"Ugh, fine," I grunted, rolling my eyes. I took the dress from her and headed to the bathroom to change.

I came out of the bathroom and walked back into the room, filled with embarrassment.

"Huh!" Kaitlin gasped as she saw me come in. "You look amazing!"

"I look like a fool," I grumbled.

"Oh, Luna stop, you look gorgeous! That dress was made for you!" She cheered. I turned to look at myself in the full body mirror we had hanging on the end of our bunkbeds. The dress had a halter top neckline which I was very thankful for. God knows I hated showing cleavage. The chain straps were surprisingly comfortable, and the dress didn't ride up like I imagined it would, even though it had a small slit on the left thigh.

"Ok, time for hair and makeup," Kaitlin cheered. She sat me down at her desk and curled my long, cherry hair into loose beach waves. She then did my makeup a little more extravagantly than I usually wore it. She gave me a bold cat eye with black eye liner, and dark red lipstick that complemented my hair.

"You look stunning." She smiled. I looked in the mirror at my reflection, stunned. I didn't even recognize myself but to my surprise, I kind of liked it.

Kaitlin got herself ready, wearing a blush pink, short dress that matched her pink feather in her hair. She also curled her long, blonde hair into loose beach waves, before painting her face perfectly with her makeup. She really was a jack of all trades with her many artistic talents.

"Ready?" she asked excitedly.

"As I'll ever be," I admitted.

We headed out of our dorm and out onto the street. Other college students flooded the streets and sidewalks, all heading toward Greek Street. We followed the crowd in excitement, as Kaitlin said hello to everyone we walked past. *She's such a social butterfly,* I thought. *I wonder what it must feel like to be so extroverted.*

We turned onto Greek Street and my eyes widened as my jaw fell open. The street was swarmed with college students, with only shoulder to shoulder breathing room. Police officers sat high on top of horses, blocking off the side streets, keeping watch on all the kids. I took a big gulp at the sight of their intimidation. Kaitlin grabbed my hand and pulled me up onto the walkway of the first house. It was a large, colonial style, white, frat house with large, black, Greek letters hanging over top the front door.

There was a group of guys playing beer pong in the front yard as we walked inside. Rap music was playing loudly throughout the house, making the walls shake to the beat. The house was filled with freshman talking with upper classmen, each one of them drinking out of red solo cups.

I followed Kaitlin past another beer pong table and into the kitchen. There was a large bowl filled to the brim with red punch.

"Here!" Kaitlin shouted to me over the music, handing me a cup. She grabbed the ladle and poured the jungle juice into my cup for me, before filling her own. "Cheers!" She smiled, clinking my cup and taking a drink. I took a sip in unison with her, then instantly gagging at the taste. It was pure vodka. Kaitlin laughed at my disgusted facial expression before taking another drink from her cup.

She grabbed my arm again, pulling me to the living room where there were two empty seats on an old, brown couch. We sat down together, in between two upperclassmen guys. I could feel the couch under me shaking to the music, as neon lights flashed through the room to the beat.

"Wow," I whispered to myself. So, this was a real college party. I took a drink from my cup, feeling a burning sensation as it ran down my throat. My cheeks flushed warmly as I gagged again at the taste.

"Not a big fan of the jungle juice, huh?" the boy next to me shouted. I was startled by the sound of his voice, almost forgetting that he was sitting next to me. I nodded in response. "I don't blame you," he continued, "it's mostly vodka, anyway." His words were slightly slurred as he spoke, his brown eyes drooping and body swaying. "You know, you're really beautiful." He complimented me, while leaning in toward me. "That dress is really working for ya."

I felt my cheeks blush at his compliment before instantly feeling a rock form in my gut. *I can't flirt with this guy. What about Eric? Oh Eric,* I thought.

I stood up quickly and shuffled through the crowd to a nearby staircase. Squeezing my way through people up the stairs, until I found a bathroom upstairs unoccupied. I ran inside, locking the door behind me. Placing my arms on the edge of the sink, looking at my reflection in the mirror. *This isn't me,* I thought to myself, *I can't do this.* My eyes welled up with tears as my arms shook. God, I miss him so much.

"Luna? Are you okay?" I heard Kaitlin knock on the outside of the door. I wiped my eyes before unlocking the door and letting her in. "Hey," she said comfortingly as she wrapped her arms around my shoulders. "Did that guy say something to you? Cause if he did, I swear I'll go kick his ass right now." I let out a small giggle at her threat.

"No, he was fine. I just feel guilty, like I'm betraying Eric," I admitted. Kaitlin turned and shuts the door behind her, blocking out the music.

"Oh, girl, I'm sorry. I didn't even think about that." She confessed, setting her cup on the bathroom counter.

"It's okay, to be honest, I'm not even sure what we really are. I mean I'd like to think of him as my boyfriend, but he lives miles away from me. We barely text because it just makes things harder for both of us and I don't know when I'm going to see him again." I confessed. I let out a big sigh, dropping my head. I stepped back and sat down on the closed toilet, resting my cheeks in my hands.

"Well, maybe it's time you asked yourself if this relationship is worth it. I mean, I hate to say it, but you sound more upset than happy. I mean like you said, you don't know when you're even going to see him again." She spoke comfortingly while hopping up onto the sink counter and taking a sip of her drink. "Maybe it's time to let him go, and focus on your dream of being an artist and going to school."

I hated hearing the words that escaped her lips, but I couldn't fight the nagging feeling that she was right.

"I think you're right," I whispered, letting out a deep sigh. "I hate it, but I think you're right."

"I know it's not what you want to hear. But the sooner you face the truth, the easier it'll be for you to move forward." She spoke. I nodded in agreement.

"I think I'm going to head home, if that's okay." I announced weakly.

"I'll come with you; I think I've had more than enough of this jungle juice." She said with a laugh.

We headed out of the bathroom arm in arm, making our way out of the house and heading for home.

When we arrived back to our dorm, changed into our pajamas and climbed into bed.

"Goodnight." I spoke to her as I turned out the light.

"Goodnight." Kaitlin yawned back.

I lay on my side, staring at the window across from me. There was a small separation in the curtain that let the glow of a street light shine into the room. I let out a deep breath before reaching for my phone. I unlocked it and went to my text messages, clicking on Eric's name.

"Hey, I know it's late, but there's something I need to tell you.

I love you. But I can't handle the long distance between us.

Not knowing when I'm going to ever see you again kills me.

And I can't continue on like this. I have to let you go." Send.

Chapter 8

I awoke the following morning to the sun streaming in through the window. My eyes were blood shot and very swollen. I must've been crying in my sleep. My head ached at the thought of last night's jungle juice. Groaning as I slowly rolled out of bed, I tried to stand up right so I could go take a shower. Kaitlin was still sound asleep in the top bunk bed, small, quiet snores escaping her.

I got out of the shower feeling alive again. The warm water rejuvenating my body with the wakeup call it desperately needed. I got myself dressed and ready for the day before heading out to the dining hall for a hot cup of coffee. I could hear it calling my name. Campus was quieter than usual this morning. Everybody was still in bed, hungover from last night's festivities.

I grabbed my coffee and breakfast and headed back to the dorm. As I turned to walk down our street, I saw two college students setting up a table on the corner. An emerald, green tablecloth with the sign "Art Club" written across it draped over the table. I stopped in my tracks, hesitant for a moment. *I'm already at an art school,* I thought. *Do I really need participate in an art club, too? What about my weekly classes? I'm already taking a heavy course load. What if I can't keep my grades up while participating in this club?* I let out a deep sigh. *Screw it.* I walked over to the table and took one of the fliers they were passing out.

"Come Join Art Club!
We meet once a week on Tuesdays,
Dive into all different types of art and creativity!" I read the flyer.

Eh, what's the worst that could happen? I thought to myself.

I walked back into my room to find a wide-awake Kaitlin blow drying her hair.

"Good morning!" She greeted me.

"Good morning," I half smiled back.

"I don't know about you, but I have a killer headache," Kaitlin admitted.

"Yeah, I had one too, but there's nothing coffee can't solve," I replied. Kaitlin let out a wholehearted laugh in response. "Hey, I got this flyer that they're passing out for an art club. Looks kind of interesting. Would you want to check it out with me?" I asked. Part of me didn't want to go if she wasn't interested. Having to force myself into a social situation each week that didn't result in a grade sounded exhausting.

"I don't know. I've actually already signed up for a photography club and an illustration club," She admitted.

"Oh, that's okay." I spoke shyly.

"Hey, you should still go, You need to get out there try new things," she comforted me.

"Hey, I try new things," I mocked. "I went to a party with you last night."

"Yeah, that I had to drag you to," she mocked back. "Come on. This is for school. It could benefit your art in so many ways. You're going."

"Yeah, yeah," I rolled my eyes.

I sat down at my desk and started to prepare for this week's classes. The rest of the weekend passed by quickly. I spent most of my time watching movies in our dorm and drinking more coffee. Tuesday afternoon came around, and I tried to find as much courage as possible to go to art club. I took a deep breath in before leaving my dorm room and heading across campus. Kaitlin was already gone at her own extracurricular activities, leaving me to push myself into a social situation.

It was held in one of the community buildings that was in the center of campus. I walked inside the front door to find a six-foot story building, swarmed with other college students. I immediately felt a rock form in my gut. I followed some signs to the third floor and finally found the right room. It was small, with only ten other people waiting inside. Quiet jazz music played as two students set up pottery wheels throughout the room. My heart ached at the sight of them. *I miss my mom,* I thought to myself. I'd been so caught up this past week with my classes and fitting in that I forgot how much I missed her.

"Luna?" A male voice called, pulling me from my thoughts. I turned to find a tall, light brown-haired boy with dark, brown eyes. *Wait a minute*, I thought, *why does he look so familiar?* "Luna, it's me, Collin, from orientation?" he explained awkwardly.

"Oh my gosh, yes, hey Collin." I replied embarrassed.

"Hey, I was wondering when I'd see you again." He smiled. My heart raced.

"Yeah, who knew it'd be so soon?" I laughed nervously.

"Well, here, come sit by me." He gestured toward two of the pottery wheels. I nodded in response and followed him to our seats. "So, how are you liking college so far?"

"It's not as bad as I thought it would be," I admitted.

"Sounds like you had high expectations for it," he mocked me.

"I guess you could say that." I felt my cheeks flushing. "Uh, what're you majoring in?"

"Illustration. I've always been into comics, and so one day I hope to design my own stories." he explained. I nodded in understanding.

"You would like my roommate; she enjoys illustration too. I'm surprised you didn't join their extracurricular group," I acknowledged.

"I thought about it, but I figured I'd enjoy a broader art club instead since I'm already spending all week taking classes for it. I didn't want to burn myself out," he explained.

"Makes sense," I replied. Collin opened his mouth to say something but was interrupted by the leader of the art club. We each received a hand full of clay and began to sculpt our projects. I fumbled with my pile as I turned on the pottery wheel, struggling to keep hold of it. Collin let's out a small chuckle at my effort.

"So, where are you from?" he questioned me.

"New York, but I've lived all over the country." I explain. I can see his body perk up at my response.

"Really? How come?" he asked. I explained my mom's economical income and its influence on where we lived. "That sounds so cool," he admitted.

"It's all right." I replied, finally starting to round out my clay.

"I grew up all over the country, too," he confessed. I turned toward him out of curiosity.

"Was your mom a starving artist too?" I mocked. He lets out a small laugh.

"No, I grew up in a military family. My mom is in the army, so we moved around all the time to live where she was stationed." he explained. My eyes widened in fascination.

"That sounds pretty cool," I admitted. "Although, I'm sorry you never got to stay in one place." Collin stopped his pottery wheel and turned toward me.

"Thanks," he spoke to me, with a melancholy look in his eyes. We continued to make small talk throughout the rest of our class time. By the time art club was over, I had successfully made a small bowl that waved around the rim, far from symmetrical. Collin took mine and placed it in the kiln alongside his. We grabbed our things and headed out of the community building together.

"Would you want to grab some coffee?" Collin asked as we walked out the front doors.

"Sure," I agreed. "There's a really good coffee cart by my dorm."

"Sweet, lead the way." I nodded in agreement as we headed across campus together. "So, of all the places you've lived, which one was your favorite?" He asked. There was only one place I had ever made roots, one place I had ever bonded with anyone. My heart began to ached.

"Uh, New York, where my mom lives now," I choked.

"How come?" Collin questioned. I took a deep breath, pondering my answer.

"It's just the first place I ever really made friends, I guess." I hesitated. Collin nodded in understanding. "What about you?" I asked quickly, trying to change the spotlight off of me.

"South Carolina, definitely." He smiled. "I got to live out my last two years of high school there and it was awesome." We arrived at the coffee cart, getting our drinks before heading turning my dorm.

"Well, this is me," I announced nervously. "Uh, thanks for walking me home."

"Yeah, no problem," he smiled. "Maybe we can do this again sometime over a study date or something." I almost choked on my coffee at his forwardness.

"Uh, yeah." I replied hesitantly. "That sounds great."

"Awesome," he smiled. "Well, I'll see you next Tuesday." He lifted his cup in a goodbye gesture before walking away. I watch after him for a moment, his baby blue T-shirt hugging his arms perfectly, not a hair out of place with his fresh new haircut. *Maybe Collin can be a fresh start,* I thought, *maybe he can help me move on from Eric. Oh, Eric.* I let out a deep sigh before heading inside my dorm.

The following afternoon, I headed to the library to study after my last class of the day. The library was ten stories tall and the further you went up, the quieter each floor got. So naturally, I went straight up the elevator to the tenth floor.

The elevator doors opened to a wide-open room, library books spread along the walls, there were college students sitting at each table in the open space. I scanned the room looking for an empty table only to find they were all occupied. Filled with disappointment I went to turn back to the elevator when out of the corner of my eye, I spotted Collin. He was sitting at a corner table with his Air Pods in, looking intensely focused on his laptop. I took in a deep breath and slowly walked across the room to him.

I approached the table, startling him from his studying. He looked up at me with a wide, genuine smile. I mouthed to him, "can I sit here?" and he nodded in response. I pulled out the chair across from him, setting up my notebooks and laptop. I put in my Air Pods and got to work studying today's lessons. I began typing out an essay from my morning class with Collin slid a piece of notebook paper to me across the table. I gave him a confused look before reaching to open it.

"I'm happy to see you" he'd written. I looked back up at him, a small smile escaping my lips. I flipped the note over, writing my response.

"I'm glad to see you too," I wrote. I folded the note back up and slid it back across the table to him. I felt like a silly thirteen-year-old girl passing notes to her friends in class. How cliché. He smiled as he read my response. He slid the note back to me after quickly writing down another message. When I reached to grab it, he caught my hand in his, slowly releasing the paper through my fingers. I felt sparks at his touch, electricity shooting up my arm. I blushed and pulled the note to me.

"Meet me in aisle 37" he wrote. I looked back at him, confused. He gave me a wink and stood up from the table, walking around the corner of the room. I paused for a moment, scanning the room to see if anyone was watching us. Luckily, everyone in the room was nose deep in their books.

I stood up slowly and walked around the corner, searching for aisle 37. It was in the back, at the very end, against the wall. I walked over to it, finding Collin in the back of the aisle, leaning his shoulder up against the wall. He looked cool, relaxed, sexy. I took a deep breath and glanced over my shoulder, checking once more that no one was watching us, before slowly walking toward him. He looked deep in my eyes, pulling another note out of his shirt pocket, gently placing it into my hand, never breaking eye contact. Butterflies stirred in my stomach; my hand shook at his touch. I looked down at the note and slowly unfolded it.

"I've wanted to kiss you, ever since I met you," he'd written. I took a big gulp before looking back up into his eyes. A smile escaped his lips as he lifted his hand, gently brushing my hair away from my face. He rested his hand on the back on my neck and placed his other hand around my waist, slowly pulling me in to him. I let out a deep breath that I didn't know I was holding in and pressed my lips against his. I lifted my hands up onto his shoulders as he kissed me back passionately. The butterflies in my gut exploded throughout my entire body. This kiss, our kiss, was electric. I pulled away slowly, stopping only inches from his face. Looking deep into his eyes, he smiled at me as I gazed upon him.

But as I observed his face, I found myself looking for someone else's expression. He leaned in slowly, pressing his lips to my ear. "We should probably get back," he whispered. I nodded shakily in response and followed him back to our seats.

Chapter 9

I worked through each of my classes in a blur. I could not stop thinking about that kiss. I was filled with both excitement and guilt about seeing Collin at art club tonight. Butterflies fluttered in my gut but I'm still in love with Eric. Why does love have to be so complicated?

I stopped at my dorm before heading to art club. Kaitlin was sitting at her desk, nose deep in homework. I tossed my bookbag on the floor and collapsed face first into the futon.

My disruption startling Kaitlin, forcing her to acknowledge my presence.

"Hey, what's going on?" She asks, turning toward me. I groan into the mattress in response. "Oh, I see. We've stopped acting our age." She mocked. I groaned at her again. She let out a small chuckle. I hear the sound of her chair scoot across the floor, just as she jumps on top of me.

"Ah!" I shout out in shock. Kaitlin grabs a pillow and starts hitting me with it. "Hey! Hey!" I call out, throwing up my hands to try to block it. She lets out a whole-hearted laugh.

"Come on cranky pants! Let's use our words and tell me why you're so grumpy." She teases. I roll my eyes before sitting up, facing her.

"I don't know what to do about Collin." I admit.

"What do you mean? I thought things were going well between you two?" She questions.

"They are but I'm still not over Eric. I feel guilty about starting something with Collin but also really excited at the same time. UGH! Tell me what to do." I pleaded.

"Well, if you're really not ready for something new with Collin, then just tell him. I mean come on you've only hung out twice, and both times were unplanned so it's not like you've even gone on a date or anything yet. Just talk to him." She consoled. I let out a deep sigh.

"Can you just talk to him for me?" I begged, hitting her shoulder playfully. Kaitlin rolled her eyes dramatically before hitting me once more with the pillow. We both cried out in laughter. *It's nice having a real friend*, I thought.

I grabbed my keycard and headed for art club, feeling my heart pounding in my chest. I small rock slowly forming in my gut the closer I walked to the community building.

I entered the classroom where the two club leaders were setting up trays with paint supplies. I small smile escaped my lips at the sight of paint.

"Hey, you." Greeted a familiar voice. I turned around to find Collin standing behind me with two coffee cups in hand. "Here, I got this for you." He hands me on of the cups.

"Oh, thank you." I replied surprised. No one has ever given me something meaningful before, especially a boy. Even if it was just a cup of coffee. "You really didn't have to."

"I wanted to." He smiles. "Want to pick our seats?"

"Sure." I nod, heading over to two empty tables. I set my coffee down and we scoot in. The leaders handed out our pottery from last week, I stare at my wonky bowl and let out a small chuckle. *How embarrassing,* I thought. We picked up our paint brushes and got to work. I dived deep into concentration, painting a monochromatic, ombre mural of blues and greens along the bowl.

"Looks like somebody's deep in thought." Collin laughed. I nearly jumped out of my skin, almost forgetting he was next to me.

"Oh, yeah, sorry. I get a little focused when I paint." I admit shyly.

"No, it's ok." He smiles. "It's cute."

I feel my cheeks heat up and turn red. *How does he have such an effect over me?* I thought.

The rest of art club passed way too quickly; I barely finish my painting in time. Collin took my bowl with his and set them over on the drying rack before we headed out together.

"Are you hungry?" He asked. "I know it's a bit early for dinner, but maybe we could grab some frozen yogurt or something?" I hesitated on my answer. *Should I just tell him now?* I thought. *Ugh, I really don't want to have this conversation.*

"Uh… yeah, frozen yogurt sounds great." I agree nervously. We head to the dining hall together, making small talk along the way.

I head to the frozen yogurt machine, pouring myself a bowl of half chocolate, half coffee flavor. Collin makes a bowl of half strawberry and half banana before following me over to a table.

"So, are you looking forward to winter break coming up?" He asks. I swallow a mouth full of frozen yogurt.

"Definitely. I mean it's still quite a few weeks away but I'm really excited to see my mom." I admitted.

"You and me both." Collin agrees. "I hate to admit it but I'm a definitely a momma's boy." He smiles.

I let out an honest laugh in response. "Hey, there's nothing wrong with that." I teased him.

"Maybe we can spend some more time together before we head home for break?" He suggests. I'm still not used to his forwardness.

"Oh, uh, yeah, about that." I hesitate, feeling my palms begin to sweat. "I wanted to talk with you about our situation."

"Oh, boy, I don't like the sound of that." Collin stirs in his seat.

"Well, I just got out of a serious relationship and to be honest, I'm just not ready to pursue anything with anyone else yet." I explain, starring down at my dessert. Collin ran his hand through his perfectly styled hair.

"Hey, that's ok, I mean, do I wish things could've worked out for us, for sure, but if you're not ready then you're not ready." He comforts. He looks down at his hands, trying to hide his disappointment.

"I'm really sorry Collin." I try to urge.

"Hey, no worries." He reaches out for my hand. "But, when you are eventually ready, I'll be waiting for you." My eyes widen, as I try to gulp the shock across my face.

"Wait? For me?" I asked shyly.

"Definitely." He winks. "You're a girl worth waiting for." He squeezes my hand gently.

"Oh, well, thank you, I guess." I stumble over my words, shocked and hesitant about what to say. Collin lets a smile escape his lips as he chuckles.

We finish our dessert quickly before heading out of the dining hall. He walks me back to my dorm, stopping at the front steps.

"Well, I'll see you around at art club." Collin suggests. He leans in and gives me a soft kiss on my cheek. "Bye Luna." He gives me his dashing smile and turns to walk away. I stand frozen, holding my breath. Wow.

I spent the next several weeks holed up in the library, studying for exams and completing homework assignments. Collin and I remained friendly, spending time together each week at art club.

Winter break finally arrived; I was beyond relieved to be finished with final exams. Kaitlin and I spent all weekend packing up our dorm room together.

"Promise you'll facetime me every day?" Kaitlin pleaded.

"Yes, I promise." I laughed. "I'll tell you all about my boring day job and my customer interactions."

"Hey, you can laugh all you want but after living together for three months, I'm going to go into Luna withdrawal," she teased me. As silly as it sounded out loud, I was really going to miss seeing Kaitlin every day, too.

I got my duffle bag packed and grabbed my very full bag of dirty laundry and took one last look at our room.

"Well, I guess I'd better head out; I don't want to miss my train," I announced. Kaitlin turned to me with a sad expression.

"Text me when you make it home, so I know you're safe," she demanded, giving me a hug.

"I promise, I will." I comforted her, hugging her back. I give her a whole-hearted smile and grabbed my bags, heading out the door.

I took a cab to the train station; it wasn't nearly as busy as I anticipated. I guess most kids were getting rides from their parents. But I didn't mind the train ride, it would give me time to read.

I snagged a cup of coffee before getting on the train. It was going to be another seven-hour trip home with several stops along the way. I couldn't wait to see my mom.

I was able to grab a seat by the window in an empty aisle, I loved when that happened. I pulled my book out of my duffle and dove into reading.

"Poughkeepsie, New York! Poughkeepsie New York!" The train employee shouted out. I jumped up, startled from his loud voice, I must've dosed off. I rubbed my eyes awake and tossed my book back into my bag. The train came to a stop, and I headed out onto the platform. With bags in hand, I headed out to the front curb of the train station, looking for my mom's old station wagon.

"Luna!" A very familiar voice cried out. I looked across the street to see my mom waving at me through the driver's side window. A huge smile filled my face. I ran across the street to her car and jumped in.

"Mom!" I cheered, throwing my arms around her shoulders.

"Oh, honey I'm so happy to see you! It's been way too long without my girl." She smiled. She brushed my hair behind my ear. "Look at you, all grown up." A car honked behind us impatiently. "Oh, don't get your panties in a wad," my mom scoffed. I let out a giggle as she put the car into drive and headed for home. As she drove through the countryside, I sat and rememorized the features of her face. She had a few extra wrinkles around her eyes, revealing her exhaustion and age. Her curly hair was full and long, framing her face. God, I was so happy to be home.

Chapter 10

I got my old job back as a barista at Starbucks and kept up on my promise to FaceTime Kaitlin every day. She was right- it's weird not seeing her after living together for a while.

I took off my apron and hung it up on the wall, getting ready to take my lunch break. I walked over to the espresso machine to make myself a drink, when out of the corner of my eye, I saw Eric walk past the store. My heart skipped a beat. I ran out from behind the counter, through the lobby and out the front door. I looked desperately through the crowd of people passing by, searching for his black jacket when I spotted him, walking across the street.

I ran after him, not noticing the taxi cabs driving through traffic. I caught up to him and placed my hand on his shoulder.

"Eric!" I exclaimed, panting. He turned around, only for it to be a stranger. A tall, dark brown, shaggy haired man in a black jacket. Not Eric. My body instantly filled with embarrassment. "Oh, God- I'm so sorry, I thought you were somebody else," I explained.

"Oh, no worries." The man shrugged. I backed away from him nervously before heading back to the store.

What is wrong with me? I thought. *He doesn't even live here anymore. Why am I still so hung up on him? I have got to get over this.* I did the walk of shame up to the front of the store when I noticed a tall, dark brown, shaggy-haired boy with bright blue eyes and a black jacket staring at me. It was Eric.

"Oh my God." I exhaled. "You're here."

"Yeah," he half whispered, "I'm here." We stood there for a moment, awkwardly gazing at each other. "I'm sorry if this is a bad time. I was actually hoping to catch you here."

"Oh, uh, I'm actually just on my lunch break so I don't have much time." I admitted. My heart skipped a beat.

"I understand," he said shyly. "Well, then are you free after work?"

"Uhm, yeah I guess so." I hesitated.

"Great, uhm, do you want to meet at Meyer's Olde Dutch Beacon? I hear it's a half decent restaurant," he suggested.

"Yeah, that sounds okay." I choked out.

"Okay, well I guess I'll see you then," he stumbled. Eric walked away awkwardly, both of us embarrassed about the conversation that had just unfolded. *Oh my God, I can't believe he's here,* I thought. *Should I be meeting him for dinner? What if that just makes me fall for him all over again? Maybe I should text him and cancel.* Well, we both know I wouldn't do that.

I finished the rest of my shift in a total fog, jumping at every sound, lost in thought. *What should I wear tonight?* I thought to myself. *Why does he want to meet me? Is there something important he wants to talk about? Maybe he's moved back here.* An endless train of thoughts, traveling at high speed with no end in sight. I have got to focus.

I headed home after work to get myself ready, my stomach beginning to fill with butterflies. I took a shower to wash off the day and curled my hair into loose, beach waves. I painted on my makeup and decided to wear something casual, as if I wasn't trying too hard, even though, I was. I put on a long sleeved, black, wool sweater with ripped, blue jeans and white combat boots. Feeling confident in my appearance, I grabbed my black purse and headed out the door.

I pulled into the parking lot of the restaurant, immediately spotting his car. I decided to pull up to the spot next to it, looking over to see Eric was waiting inside. We smiled awkwardly at each other before getting out of our cars.

"Hey," he greeted me.

"Hey," I half smiled in response.

"Shall we?" He asked, gesturing toward the entrance. I nodded in response and headed inside. We were seated right away in a corner booth. We placed our orders with the server, finishing any distraction left from deterring us to actual talk.

"So," I spoke out, breaking the ice. "Why did you want to meet?"

"Honestly, because I missed seeing you," he admitted.

"Oh," I exhaled. "I've missed you, too." I looked down at my hands in my lap, pulling at the sleeves of my sweater.

"Uhm, how's college?" Eric asked, clearing his throat from the tension.

"Oh, uh, it's fine. I just finished final exams, which sucked, but otherwise good, I guess."

"That's good," he stuttered, shifting in his seat. I was glad I wasn't the only who was nervous.

"How's Colorado?" I questioned.

"It's been good, but I uh… actually just moved back here," he admitted coolly. I perked up instantly.

"You moved back?" I questioned. "Why?"

"My sister is sick," he whispered, dropping his head. "She has leukemia."

My heart sank. A long pause grew between us. Eric still looked away, unable to meet my gaze.

"I'm so sorry," I finally exhaled. I reached out across the table slowly, pausing for a moment before grabbing his hand, squeezing it gently. "What do the doctors say?"

"It's stage four and she's not responding to treatments." Tears welled up in his eyes. "They say it's a matter of time," he choked.

"Oh, Eric. What can I do?" I cried.

"I don't know. Luna," He whimpered. "Just having you here makes everything better."

"I'm not going anywhere." I promised. "I'll be here for anything you need."

Eric sniffled and nodded in acknowledgement. I wiped the tears from my eyes. Both of us were unable to speak. Seeing him so upset broke my heart all over again. There was nothing worse than seeing a guy cry, especially one that you love.

We eat our dinner mostly in silence, making small talk occasionally. Eric paid the bill, and he followed me back out to the parking lot. I unlocked my car and leaned my back up against it, facing Eric.

"I'm happy to come home on the weekends to help with your sister," I offered. "I can do my homework on the train ride and drop my extracurriculars to make time to study."

"No." Eric shook his head and crossed his arms, leaning his back up against his car. "No, school is too important. You're not wasting all of your free time traveling back and forth for me," He disagreed.

"Eric, I want to help you, let me help you." I pleaded, taking a step toward him.

"Luna, I would love nothing more than to accept your help," he admitted.

"Okay, then let me." I countered.

"But your education is too important. I can't ask you to completely change your schedule and your life for me. It's too selfish. It wouldn't be fair," he argued.

"Who's to say what is fair? It's my life. Let me be the one to decide how to manage it," I fought back.

"You are free to do whatever you want in life, Luna. But you can't throw it away on me and my family problems. You don't deserve that," he said firmly.

"I don't care!" I shouted.

"But I do!" Eric shouted back. We both take a breath. "I do care, Luna. I love you for wanting to help and support me. But I need to do this on my own."

I let out a deep sigh at his words. How could I possibly fight that?

"Fine," I exhaled. "If you want me to stay out of it then I will." I looked down at my feet, defeated. Eric took a step toward me and lifted my chin gently with his finger. He looked deep into my eyes, observing my face. "I don't like fighting with you," He breathed out.

"I don't like fighting with you either." I admitted. I let myself fall forward into his chest as he wrapped his arms around me. "At least keep me updated," I pleaded onto his shoulder. "You know, like let me know what's going on."

"I will." Eric whispered.

"You promise?" I whispered back.

"I promise." He comforted. We held each other for a moment longer, before exiting the embrace. "I should get home," he announced. I nodded in response. "I'm happy I got to see you."

"I'm happy I got to see you, too," I admitted softly. Eric gave me a soft smile before getting into his car. I stood still beside mine, watching him pull out of the parking lot and out of view. I let out a deep sigh, that I didn't know I was holding in. I turned to get into my car and head for home. I drove in silence. I stared out at the open road in front of me, unaware of what the future was going to bring.

Chapter 11

Winter break passed in a haze. Between working non-stop and the unbearable silence from Eric, I couldn't concentrate on anything.

I took the train back to school, meeting Kaitlin at our dorm right after lunch time.

"Hey! Oh, my gosh, you're finally back!" Kaitlin cheered, greeting me with a huge hug, before I was even in the door.

"Hey, I'm back." I replied, returning her hug.

"Have you heard from Eric at all?" she asked. My heart ached at his name.

"No," I muttered, tossing my bags on my bed and beginning to unpack.

"Maybe it's for the best. I mean, he does have a lot on his plate, and so do you. Plus I think he made himself pretty clear about not wanting you involved." She explained.

"Yeah, but radio silence? I mean, he promised to at least keep me updated," I pleaded.

"I know. It'll be ok." She comforted me by tapping my back gently.

"I know. Let's just talk about something else," I shrugged. Just as the words escaped my lips, there was a knock on our door. "Were you expecting somebody?" I asked Kaitlin. She shook her head no, confused.

I walked over to the door and glanced through the peep hole. It was Collin. I took in a deep breath, trying to quickly straighten up my sweatpants and comb out my messy hair with my fingers.

"Hey, what're you doing here?" I greeted Collin as I opened the door halfway.

"Hey! I hope this is a good time. I figured you guys were moving back in, so I thought I'd stop by," he explained.

"Oh, uh, yeah, come on in," I hesitated, opening the door the rest of the way. Collin walked in and surveyed the room.

"Wow, your room is really nice and clean," he acknowledged.

"You can thank Kaitlin for that. She's the neat freak," I admitted.

"You must be Collin." Kaitlin greeted, offering out a hand.

"Oh, yeah, hey, you must be the roommate." Collin replied. Kaitlin smiled and shook her head, her long, blonde hair falling into her face.

"Well, you guys look busy, so I won't overstay my welcome, but I just wanted to give you this." Collin announced. He turned toward me and handed me a small, emerald-green box wrapped with a perfect red bow.

"What is this?" I asked confused, reaching out to take the box from him.

"What's it look like?" He chuckled. "It's a Christmas gift."

Kaitlin covered her mouth with her hands from behind Collin, trying to hold in her gasp. I gently pulled off the red ribbon and opened the green jewelry box to find a beautiful, dainty, silver bracelet. A colored charm of a painter's palette hung from the chain. I held up the bracelet, stunned, admiring its detail.

"I don't know what to say," I gasped. "Thank you, Collin. You really didn't need to do this."

"I know, but I wanted to." Collin smiled. He stepped toward and pulled me in for a hug. I wrapped my arms around his shoulders as he pressed his lips to my ear. "Merry late Christmas, Luna," he whispered.

"Merry late Christmas," I choked out. Collin pulled away from me, giving me his devilish wink before heading for the door.

"I'll catch you guys later," he announced.

"It was nice meeting you!" Kaitlin replied. Collin give her a friendly wave and closed the door behind himself.

"Oh. My. God!" Kaitlin exclaimed. "He got you a bracelet!"

I stood stunned, unable to reply.

"Hello! Luna! Why are you holding off on that guy? He's so hot and generous, I mean if you don't date him I will!" She teased me.

"Yeah, yeah, I know he's really great but I'm just not ready. I mean Eric is still in my life and if he is, it's not fair for me to start something with Collin." I explained.

"Start? Honey, you're way past starting something with him. I mean, hello!" She exclaimed, pointing at the jewelry box. "Besides, Eric's giving you the silent treatment. How much is he really in your life?"

"I hate when you're right," I scoffed, letting out a deep sigh.

Kaitlin and I finished unpacking our things and prepared for tomorrow's classes.

"Oh, hey, didn't you want to talk to your guidance counselor before class tomorrow?" Kaitlin reminded me.

"Oh, shoot." I snatched my phone to check the time. "Her office is only open for thirty more minutes; do you think she'll still see me?"

"If you run," she encouraged me.

I grabbed my key card and ran out the door, heading for the administrative building across campus.

I luckily made it in time to change one my class times from morning to afternoon, giving myself the ability to sleep in on Tuesdays and Thursdays.

As I walked out her office, I passed by a bulletin board with a neon yellow paper pinned to it. I stopped in my tracks, allowing it to catch my eye.

"Want to study at the Royal College of Art in London?
Apply to win a scholarship to study abroad for the summer!
Plus, win $10,000 dollars! Apply today!"

Oh. My. God. A chance to study at the most prestigious art school in the world? *How could I not sign up for this?* I thought to myself. I took the flyer off of the bulletin and took it back to the dorm.

With only one month to prepare a piece of artwork to submit to win, I needed to prepare immediately. I got back to my room and tucked into my desk. I pulled out my drawing pad and got straight to work on ideas of what to paint. I lifted my pencil and stared at the blank piece of paper. Nothing. My mind went blank. Not a single idea popped into my head. I tossed my pencil in frustration. *What am I going to do?* I thought. *I can't think of anything.*

I pulled out my laptop and began researching famous paintings, Da Vinci, Van Gogh, Picasso, all of their work popping up instantly. I went down a rabbit hole, studying each piece, each paint stroke, each color. But still, nothing.

In frustration, I decided to put my pad away and sleep on it. I changed into my pajamas, set my alarm on my phone and climbed into bed.

I spent the following day flowing from class to class and brainstorming my scholarship submission. I was still unable to think of a single idea.

I came home from my last class and through my bookbag onto the futon in annoyance.

"What's up with you?" Kaitlin questioned.

"I don't know what to paint. I've thought and thought about it but nothing. Literally nothing!" I shouted out.

"Well, maybe that's the problem, you're thinking too much," she replied. I let out a deep sigh.

"Yeah, maybe you're right," I admitted.

"Why don't you set up your easel and just see what comes to you?" she offered.

I let an amused expression overcome my face. I shrugged and began to set up my supplies. I placed an extra-large canvas that was half my size onto my easel and sat in front of it on my stool. I stared at the blank, white surface. Grabbing my paint brush, I dipped it into the black paint and let my hand paint at its own will.

Before I knew it, five hours had passed. I had painted a rough outline of a dirt path down the center of the painting. The path broke into a fork with the right side leading toward a city that resembled London. And the left side of the path leading toward a thick wooded area, with a large tree stump. The image was clear. The decision was not.

Chapter 12

Today is the day. I gently wrapped my painted canvas in a sheet and carried it out of the dorm, heading for the community building. Weaving in and out of students as I walked across campus, I was careful not to let anyone or anything touch my painting.

I arrived at the community building and made my way up the escalator to the third floor. There was a sign pointing toward a grand ballroom for the art show submissions for the London scholarship committee. I took a deep breath and walked inside. There were dozens of rows of beautiful artwork. Paintings, sculptures, photography and so much more. My painting felt very small next to these magnificent projects.

A volunteer took me over to where I would be setting up my artwork, there was an easel in place waiting for me. I placed my painting on the stand and gently removed the cloth, revealing the masterpiece. It was my best work yet. The volunteer gasped at my reveal, complimenting me on my talent. I gave her a soft smile and my gratitude. There was also a sign next to my artwork with my name and class year. It felt so weird seeing my work presented so professionally. I had competed in art shows before but nothing of this magnitude.

I took one last look before leaving to head back to the dorm, feeling confident but a bit overshadowed.

I spent the next three weeks finishing up final exams and preparing for spring break. In each of my classes the other students discussed going to Florida for vacation. I couldn't imagine a worse way to spend my time.

Drunk college students running around naked, screaming and shouting about stupid things. How awful.

Kaitlin and I were finishing up packing out dorm on the last day of classes.

"I'm really going to miss you." Kaitlin announced.

"I know, but we'll be back before we know it. It's not like winter break when we were gone for two and a half months." I comforted her, tossing another sweater into my bag.

"You're right, plus we'll be able to FaceTime again." She smiled. I gave her a soft smile back. "Oh, I almost forgot my laundry, I'll be back." Kaitlin headed out, making her way to the laundry room, closing the door behind her when I hear a ding from my laptop. I open it to find a new email in my inbox.

Dear Ms. Luna Hart,
We are pleased to inform you that you have made the Dean's list of academics for the semester. Congratulations.

"Oh my gosh! No way!" I cried out. I set the laptop down and did a little happy dance in celebration. *I can't believe it,* I thought, *all that hard work finally paid off.*

A knock at the door pulled me out of my glee.

"Kaitlin, did you forget your key card again?" I called out. I swung open the door to find Collin standing in the doorway.

"Hopefully not, but at least you're here in case she did," he teased.

"Uh, hey, sorry I obviously thought you were Kaitlin. Uh, come in." I hesitated. He gave me a charming smile and walked into the room, sitting on the futon.

"Are you guys packing up to head home for break?" Collin asked.

"We are," I responded, gesturing to my duffle bag. "Are you going to Florida like everyone else?" I teased him.

"Uh, yeah, I actually am," he chuckled. "A couple of my guys on my floor invited me to go with them, so I figured, why not?"

"Oh geez," I replied rolling my eyes.

"Hey, now, it's not that bad, besides I don't plan on drinking that much anyway," he admitted.

"You say that now, but the moment you get there, everyone is going to be peer pressuring you, and it's a lot easier to say that you're going to say no, rather than actually doing it," I antagonized him.

"True, but I can handle myself," he smirked coolly. I stood there for a moment, holding his gaze. He really did have deep brown eyes, almost a little hazel. My computer dings and pulled me away from our stare.

"Oh, I should probably check that. I made the Dean's list so it's probably another email about it from administration." I announced awkwardly.

"What? You made the Dean's list? Dude that's amazing!" He cheered.

"Thanks." I chuckle. I opened my email to find another new message, only this one isn't from the college administration. It was from the London Scholarship Association. My heart dropped. My breath caught in my throat. Oh, my God.

"Is everything okay?" Collin asked, seeing my scared and startled expression.

"Uh, it's an email from the London Scholarship Committee. They've finally announced the winner," I explained breathlessly.

"Well? Open it," Collin encouraged, standing up and approaching my side. I took a deep breath in and clicked on the message.

'Dear Ms. Luna Hart,
    We are happy to announce that you have won the Royal College of Art and Design Scholarship in London England!'

I screamed out as I read the first line of the message.

"Oh, my God! Oh, my God! Oh, my God!" I shouted, jumping up and down. Collin picked me up and spun me around the room, crying out in joy.

"Oh my God, Luna, this is amazing!" A burst of laughter escaped me as he spun me around the room. Collin set me back down on my own two feet but didn't remove his hands from my waist. We smiled at each other, laughing breathlessly.

"Congratulations Luna, you deserved this," Collin smiled. He lifted his hand and brushed my hair behind my ear. He held my gaze, and stared deeply into my eyes. I felt my hands shake as they rested on his shoulders.

"Collin." I whispered. He leaned in slowly, never breaking our gaze. He paused for a moment, inches from my face, glancing down at my lips before looking back into my eyes.

"Luna," he whispered before leaning in all the way. I closed my eyes and just as our lips brushed against each other's, my phone rang out. I jumped back from Collin, startled by the sound.

"Oh, uh, sorry," I apologized awkwardly. I reached for my phone that was sitting on my desk to check the caller ID. It was Eric. My heart dropped. "Um, I should probably get this," I announced, turning back to Collin.

"Oh, yeah, sure. I'll just let myself out. Have a good spring break," he replied shyly. I could tell he was disappointed.

Collin closed the door behind him when I answered the phone.

"Hello?" I answered. There was no response. "Hello? Eric?" Nothing. I'm about to hang up when I begin to heard soft sobs. "Eric? Is that you?" I asked gently.

"Luna." I heard him cry. "Luna, she's dead." My stomach clenched.

"Oh, Eric, I'm so sorry. I'm so sorry." I comforted him, falling back onto my bed. "Where are you?"

"At the hospital," he cried. "I have to fill out a bunch of stupid paperwork that I don't even understand," he scoffed. His sobbing began to worsen.

"Oh, Eric, are you there alone? Why not just have your dad fill out the paperwork?" I ask.

"He's not here," he explained angerly. My heart sank. "And now I have to plan for a funeral, which I don't know how to do and I'm just so-" his voice cuts off as he cried uncontrollably. "I can't believe she's gone," he sobbed.

"Eric, I'm coming home tomorrow morning. We'll figure this out, okay? You and me, I'll help plan the funeral, and we'll get everything sorted, okay?" I comforted him.

He paused for a moment before answering. "Okay," he exhaled.

I woke up before sunrise the following morning, catching the earliest train available. I didn't sleep a wink all night, my thoughts raced continuously. I hoped to rest my eyes on the train, but I was still too wired to rest.

The train ride was excruciating. Minutes felt like hours. I felt like I was never going to make it home. I was so eager to be at Eric's side, time seemed to slow to a lull.

I finally arrived at my stop where my mom was impatiently waiting for me. She knew I was in a rush, so I hopped in the car, and we sped off from the station, racing for home.

My mom drove me straight to the school, driving most of the way in silence. I was too stressed to speak. She pulled into the parking lot where I immediately spotted Eric's car. I jumped out of the passenger seat before the car even came to a complete stop.

Running across the parking lot at a sprint, heading straight for the woods. I wove between bushes and trees, my heart pounding as I raced for the tree stump. I came running around the corner when I stopped in my tracks. He was here. Eric jumped up from the tree stump and ran into my arms.

He buried his face into my neck and sobbed hysterically. I wrapped my arms around him, hugging him tighter than I'd ever hugged anyone before. He wrapped his arms around me, with his fingers digging into my back. I felt his knees shake.

"It's okay." I whispered into his ear. "I'm here now."

Chapter 13

I drove Eric back to the house in silence. He leaned his head against the passenger side window, gazing out at the world passing by.

I pulled into the driveway and parked the car. Eric grabs my bags and helps carry my packed belongings inside the house.

"Hey! You're finally home!" My mom greeted us. "Oh, Eric, Luna told me the news about your sister. I'm so sorry sweetie." She gives him a large, sympathetic hug as Eric falls into her arms, welcoming her embrace. They stood there for a moment before Eric helped me carry my bags to my bedroom.

"What do you want to order for dinner?" I asked. "Does anything sound good?"

"Nah, I'm not really hungry." Eric replied, as he collapsed down on to my bed, kicking off his shoes. He tugged the blankets out from under him and pulled them up over his head. A smile escaped my lips. I loved how comfortable he was around me.

"Hey, come out from under there," I teased him, sitting on the edge of the bed. Eric groaned in response. I grabbed the blankets and pulled them back down to his waist. His dark hair was in disarray. Eric gently grabbed my hand and interlaced his fingers with mine.

"I missed you." He whispered.

"I missed you, too." I whispered back. Still holding my hand, Eric pulled me into him and gently pressed his lips against mine. Everything inside me told me to pull away, but I gave into my desperation. I kissed him back passionately, missing the taste of his lips. I pulled away slowly, locking my gaze with his. He lifted my fingers to his mouth and kissed each of them lightly.

"Would it be okay if I slept for a while? I haven't slept since the hospital and I'm so tired," he admitted.

"Of course," I comforted him, as I ran my fingers through his hair. "I'll just go read out in the living room with my mom."

I turned to stand up from the bed when Eric grabbed my arm to stop me. "No, please stay with me. I can't sleep without you," he pleaded. I paused for a moment, dumb struck by his bluntness.

I gave him a small nod and crawled into the bed beside him. Eric lifted the blankets up to my shoulder and pulled me into his chest. I wrapped my arms around him and buried my face into his neck.

"I love you, Luna," he whispered, rubbing his thumb along the middle of my back. My breath caught in my throat.

"I love you, too." I whispered back. I closed my eyes, listening to his heartbeat slowly as his body began to relaxed. I spent so much time trying to move on from him that I forgot how much I missed sleeping with him.

Having his arms around me, listening to him breath slowly, in and out. He was so warm and strong but gentle and tender all the same.

I awoke to Eric slowly stretching. Letting out a large yawn, I rolled over to grab my phone. It was 10 a.m.

"Oh my gosh, we slept through all of yesterday and through the night," I gasped. "I guess we were both pretty tired," I laughed.

"I always sleep well when I sleep with you." Eric let out a small chuckle as a smirk spread across his face. God, I missed that sexy smile.

He pulled me back into him and kissed me. My lips responded intensely, craving him. I ran my hands over his body, feeling his muscles flex and contract. He squeezed my hips tightly, craving more of me. I slowly slipped my hands under the hem of his shirt, gently lifting it up. But Eric quickly stopped me.

"We should probably get some breakfast," he announced breathlessly. I nodded in agreement, embarrassed for being so physically forward, and crawled out of bed. He followed me out of my bedroom and out into the kitchen.

"Good morning," my mom greeted us. She handed us each a cup of coffee.

"Morning," we both muttered in unison, sipping on our drinks.

"What're you guys up to today?" she questioned. Eric looked at me with a painful expression. "Uh, well, we're going to have to start planning the funeral."

I spoke shyly. "Could you help?" I asked her.

"Of course. I can call the local funeral director if you guys want to call a caterer to set up a tent out back to supply food for people," she explained.

"Oh, you don't have to host the wake. I can find somewhere else to do it," Eric pleaded.

"Oh, I wouldn't dream of it! We're happy to have it here," she explained.

"Thank you, Sammy. I'm very grateful," Eric replied. She gave him a sympathetic smile. Eric and I headed back to my room to make phone calls. He climbed back into my bed as I grabbed my phone. I sat in my white, fluffy chair in the corner of my room, next to the window. Eric fell back asleep as I began calling local caterers.

After talking to several companies, I finally found an Italian restaurant that was able to cater for us. I set up a date and time for them to arrive at the house this coming weekend.

The rest of the after was spent reading in my chair as Eric slept through the day. Grief must be exhausting.

We awoke the morning of the funeral, both of us moving slowly in silence. Eric put on his best suit, and I wore a long, black maxi dress with lace sleeves. I picked out a pearl necklace my mom had given me for my sixteenth birthday. I've never worn them before, but this occasion felt appropriate. Eric stepped toward me, taking the necklace from my hand, gently wrapping it around my neck and clasping it shut for me. I turned back toward him and straightened up his tie.

"We can do this," I whispered. I placed my hand under his chin, lifting his gaze to meet mine. "You can do this." He stared deep into my eyes, longing and sorrow filled his face. He pulled me into his embrace and hugged me tightly, letting out a deep sigh before we turned to leave.

The funeral passed in a blur. It was small with a few family members and some of Eric's old friends. Although, I did finally got to put a face to his father's name. He stumbled in an hour into the service and was quickly escorted out by a family member before Eric could see him. The last thing anyone needed was a fight to break out.

I stayed by Eric's side the entire service. He held my hand for most of the time, needing support both physically and mentally.

All of the guests came back to my house and settled into our backyard. The catering team set up an extra-large, white tent that covered our entire small space. Matching white tables and chairs filled the tent with a buffet for the guests to serve themselves. It was quiet, small, and reserved.

I made Eric a plate, but he never ate a bite, just greeted everyone who repeatedly came up to him sharing their condolences.

My mom and I cleaned up after everyone had left. I showed Eric to my room and tucked him into my bed to rest. He slept through the rest of the day and into the evening.

After the funeral passed, it was time to head back to school as spring break was ending. The last thing I wanted to do was say goodbye to Eric. We both were secretly dreading this moment.

We woke up early in the morning. Eric packed my bags into his car, and we headed off to campus. I offered to take the train, but Eric insisted on driving me back himself. We drove in silence. Both of us were afraid of saying goodbye, as if saying it out loud would make it real.

As we passed over the New York border, exhaustion waved over me. I was so busy taking care of Eric that I forgot to take a moment for myself. I felt my eyes slowly growing heavier, allowing myself to fall into a deep sleep.

"Hey, Luna, we're here," Eric whispered as he rubbed my shoulder gently. I lifted my head up and let out a big yawn.

"I'm sorry. I must've dozed off," I told him, lifting my arms for a big stretch. "I hope the drive wasn't too boring for you."

"Nah, it was peaceful seeing you sleep." He smiled. We got out of the car and grabbed my bags out of the back seat. Eric set them on top of the trunk and pulled me into his arms for a hug. I wrapped my arms around his shoulders as he buried his face into my neck.

He let out a deep sigh and kissed my neck gently. Goose bumps stood up from the touch of his lips. "I don't want to let you go," he whispered. I took a deep inhale of his cologne before slowly pulling away.

"I don't want to say goodbye," I whispered back. He lifted his hand and brushed my hair behind my ear.

"Come with me," he pleaded. "I know you've said no before but things are different now. It's just you and me. And you are it for me, Luna. Please, you can transfer and go to college out there, and we can make a life for ourselves. You can paint the mountains, and I'll go back to school to be a welder, and we'll be happy and in love. Please baby, come with me." My heart sank. He'd never called me that before.

"Eric," I exhaled.

"Please Luna, just be with me," he begged, placing both hands on my shoulders.

"Eric, I can't-"

"Yes, you can. You can, Luna."

"I'm going to London," I blurted out. Shock filled Eric's face. He dropped his hands and took a step away.

"What?" he whispered.

"I've been offered a scholarship to study in London for the summer." I explained. "And I really want to go." He looked down at the ground, cracking his knuckles. He couldn't meet my gaze, breathing deeply.

"Well, I guess this is it then," he exhaled.

"Eric-"

"No, Luna. You need to go. As much as I want you, you need to go," he exhaled. He grabbed my hands and pulled me back into his embrace. "I'll wait for you." he whispered.

Eric lets me go and turned to get into his car.

"I love you, Luna," he said over his shoulder. I stepped forward and placed my hand on his back.

"I love you too, Eric." I cried, feeling the tears begin to stream down my cheeks. He opened the car door and climbed inside. Turning toward me with tears in his eyes, before pulling away from the curb and driving away from me. Again.

Chapter 14

I sat on the tree stump, listening to the leaves dance in the wind. Nature was resprouting from the harsh winter. The world was coming back to life. I took in a deep inhale, allowing my shoulders to drop, releasing my pent-up tension. This was my favorite place.

I opened my eyes to the sound of a train horn blaring behind me, I was suddenly at the train station, with a boarding ticket that read "London".

Wait, no, I was supposed to be in the woods. Why was I there? I squeezed my eyes shut tightly, counting to three before opening them again. I was on a plane. I tried unclipping my seatbelt, but it wouldn't budge.

"Help! Help!" I shouted. But the strangers around me didn't move or acknowledge my screams. They began to fade into blurry, black figures.

"Help! Please! This isn't what I want!" I screamed, still pulling at my seatbelt. I began to suffocate, clawing at my neck when suddenly, I shoot up in bed, startled awake from my alarm. I let out a loud groan and collapsed back onto my pillow.

"Did you have the same nightmare again?" Kaitlin asked from her bunk above me.

"Yes," I groaned. "It's been every night for weeks."

"I know. I wake up to your screams," she admitted.

"I'm sorry." I exhaled, pulling my comforter up over my head.

"You're going to be late if you don't get up, ya know," Kaitlin spoke sternly. I groaned at her observation.

"It's just Drawing 101. How much could I really miss?" I asked.

Kaitlin tossed her pillow at my head.

"Ow!" I shouted from under my covers.

"Oh, please, like my pillow could hurt you," she chuckled.

"Just leave me here to die," I wined.

"Don't be so dramatic. Get your butt up and go to class," she teased as she crawled down from her bunk.

I rolled my eyes and slowly stood up out of bed, stretching my hands above my head. I sat at my desk and opened my makeup mirror, observing the dark circles under my eyes. It was already halfway through spring semester, and every night since I'd moved back in, I'd had the same nightmare. *I want to go to London,* I thought. *Don't I? This is a huge opportunity; how could I pass it up?*

I went to class, running late from exhaustion. The morning line at the coffee cart seemed longer today than usual. Figures.

By late afternoon, it was time for art club. Things remained solid between Collin and me after we almost kissed. He still gave me his devilish smile.

I walked into the art room and took my usual seat next to him.

"Nice bracelet," he teased, looking down at the gift he'd given me.

"You know you say that every time." I mocked him.

"You know, you tell me that every time," he teased. "You look extra tired today. Didn't get much sleep last night?"

"Thanks for pointing out my imperfections." I rolled my eyes.

"Sorry." Collin chuckled nervously. "Are you okay? You seem kind of on edge?"

"Yeah sorry. Like you said, I'm just tired. I'm ready for the semester to end," I admitted.

"You and me both. My professors are already discussing final exam prep," he replied.

"Mine too. As quickly as the semester is flying by, it still somehow feels like it's dragging on slowly." "What a paradox." Collin laughed.

The leader of the group passed out watercolor and paint brushes with a small canvas. My heart leaped at the sight of paint. I took my brush and got to work painting a turquoise butterfly with black details. It was beautiful. The paint bled in all the right places.

"Hey, you want to grab coffee after this? I know a great spot we could study," Collin asked.

My mind immediately thought of the last time we studied together. I felt my heart begin to race. "Oh, uh, sure." I hesitated. I still felt like I was cheating on Eric, even though I well know we weren't together. But Eric had said he'd wait for me. *What do I do?* I thought to myself. My heart longed for Eric, but I couldn't deny the butterflies in my stomach fluttering with Collin's every word.

Maybe I should go to London. I can clear my mind of both of them and figure out who I really want.

Art club came to an end and with my painting in hand, I followed Collin out of the room and out to the coffee cart. It was a beautiful spring day. Birds chirped as they flew from tree to tree. Blooms popped from bushes and tulips had begun sprouting from the ground. The monochromatic colors poured life into my soul, giving me purpose again.

We got our coffees and headed over to a massive oak tree that overshadowed a large, grassy area.

"Shall we?" Collin asked as he sat down on the grass, leaning his back up against the tree trunk.

What is it with men and trees? I thought.

I sat down beside him, tossing my bookbag beside me, bumping my shoulder against his. I gave him an awkward smile, almost embarrassed by our touch. I pulled my binders out of my bag and got to work, beginning to study for finals.

We sat in silence for over an hour, exchanging the occasional glance.

"So, we never talked about that day, you know, when I gave you your Christmas gift," Collin spoke nervously. "I feel like you kind of pretended it never happened."

"Oh, yeah, I don't know why. I guess I was just nervous or something." I admitted shyly.

"Do I still make you nervous?" he asked quietly, turning his body toward mine. I felt my heart in my throat.

"Uh, yeah." I hesitated. He reached his hand out and brushed my hair behind my ear.

"I told you I'd wait for you, Luna," he whispered. "Are you ready for me yet?"

I broke away from his gaze, pulling at the grass.

"Um, I'm not sure." I confessed.

Collin placed his hand under my chin, pulling my gaze back to his, and looked down at my lips. He leaned in slowly and kissed me gently. I lifted my arms and wrapped my hands around his neck, pulling him in closer. Our kiss turned intense and passionate as he placed his hands my hips, grabbing on to me firmly. His lips move away from my mouth and kiss their way along my cheek and to my ear.

"Are you still unsure?" he whispers breathlessly. I pull away from him slowly.

"I need you to wait a little longer." I blurted out, unaware of the words escaping my lips. A surprised expression filled Collin's face.

"Can I ask why?" he questioned. I looked down at my hands, pulling at the sleeves of my black sweatshirt.

"I'm still getting over someone else." I whispered, afraid of his response.

Collin let out a deep exhale and runs his hands through his perfectly styled hair. "Okay." He finally spoke.

"Okay?" I asked confused.

"Okay, I'll wait until you're ready," he explained. I reached out and grabbed his hand, interlacing his fingers with mine.

"Thank you." I replied, astonished by his patience.

He brushed my hair away from my face and gave me a soft smile before we turned back to our books. We studied together for another hour before the sun began to set.

Collin walked me back to my dorm as the sky lit up lavender and magenta. Collin hummed a song as we stopped to admire the sunset.

"What're you singing?" I ask.

"All of me." He smiled. My breath caught in my throat; I felt the heat rise in my cheeks. I smiled as I turned away from him, trying to hide my blushing expression.

We approached my dorm and stopped at the front steps.

"Well, I guess this is goodnight." I announced.

"Yeah, goodnight, my Luna." Collin smiled, and he leaned in and kisses me on the cheek before giving me his devilish wink. He turned to walk away, as I stood there, breathlessly.

Chapter 15

Finals passed obnoxiously slow, not that I could focus on any of them. My nightmares consisted despite every attempt to get a peaceful night's sleep. How terrific.

It didn't help that Collin filled my brain. I could barely focus on packing for London with the thought of his devilish smirk. I envied the taste of his lips again, but I couldn't wait for a three-month break from him at the same time.

"I almost forgot my laundry again," Kaitlin announced as she came into our room, laundry basket in hand.

I snapped out of my head and quickly turned back to my duffle bag.

"You and your damn laundry I swear." I teased her.

She rolled her eyes back at me in response. "I can't believe it's actually summer break! I expect a postcard each week, by the way. And they better be from different places you visit, because you'd better not just whole up in your apartment or whatever the whole three months you're there," Kaitlin scolded.

"Yeah, yeah, I know," I mocked her, feeling nausea brew in my stomach.

"Seriously, though, are you okay? You don't seem too excited about going to London?" she asked.

"Yeah, I'm just tired, I guess," I replied shyly. Kaitlin stepped next to me and placed her hand on my forearm.

"Hey, you know you can talk to me," she comforted me.

"Yeah, I know. I'm sorry. I don't mean to be so cranky. I just miss Eric, I still haven't heard from him since spring break after the funeral, but Collin is so great and kind and patient and funny and I'm just, lost." I admitted to her.

"I know," Kaitlin comforted me, turning me toward her, and pulling me in for a hug.

"I'm really going to miss you," I sighed.

"I'm going to miss you, too, Luna," Kaitlin replied. She gives me a soft smile before we both got back to packing up our things.

As I gazed around the dorm room, it felt so empty without all of our belongings filling it. The walls were bare, the closets were empty, the bunk beds were stripped. I hated it. This dorm room has been home for the last nine months. How was I supposed to just pack up and leave? I was never coming back.

Next year Kaitlin and I would be somewhere else. I felt myself begin to well up. This transition would be much more difficult than I thought it would be.

My phone dinged with a text message from my mom, letting me know she had arrived on campus. Kaitlin and I turned in our keys to the resident assistants and carried the last of our things out to the front steps of our dorm building.

"Well, my parents are just a few cars down that way, so I guess this is it," Kaitlin announced, pointing down the street. She and I hugged one last time before she started down the sidewalk.

My mom pulled the station wagon up to the curb and jumped out of the driver's seat.

"My Luna!" she cheered. With wide open arms, she pulled me into her embrace. "Oh, how I've missed you."

"I've missed you, too." I smiled. She brushed my hair behind my ear and kissed my cheek. We started unloading the car with my several bags.

"Luna!" A familiar voice call from behind me. I turn around to find Collin jogging toward me.

"Collin, hey." I greeted him awkwardly. He ran up to me, out of breath. "Is something wrong?" I asked.

"Oh, no. I just wanted to see you before you leave," he admitted breathless. I brushed my hair nervously with my fingers before remembering my mom stood behind me.

"Oh, this is my mom, Sammy. Mom, this is my friend, Collin," I introduced them.

"Collin, it's so nice to meet you," my mom greeted him with a warm hug.

"It's a pleasure to meet you, Sammy," Collin welcomed her embrace warmly.

"I'll give you two a minute," my mom announced. She grabbed the trash we'd brought out and headed toward the dumpsters.

"So I'm about to head home," I told Collin shyly to Collin.

"Yeah, me too. My folks are waiting for me back at my dorm," he replied.

"Oh, well, I guess this is goodbye then," I hesitated.

"Yeah." Collin smiled. "But before you go, there was something I needed to tell you." He admitted.

"Okay?" I asked, confused.

He looked down at the ground and cracked his knuckles before he looked back up at me, looking deep into my eyes.

"Luna, I think I'm in love with you," he announced. "I've been in love with you since the moment I saw you at orientation in line at the coffee cart. I'm in love with your smile, you're red hair, your dry sarcasm. You're amazing, and I'm in love with you. I can't believe how many times I'm saying it." He smiled nervously.

I'm stunned. I can't breathe. Am I deaf? I can feel myself choke. I can't speak. Oh, my, God I can't speak.

"Right now is about the time you say something." Collin chuckled nervously, running his hand through his hair.

"Collin." I choked. He looked deep into my eyes, anxiously awaiting my response. "Collin, I'm in love with someone else," I whispered. Collin dropped his head, closing his eyes and clenching his fists. "Collin, I-" he turned and walked away from me, wordless and devastated, cold. "Collin, wait!" I called after him.

He jogged away, running from me as fast as he possibly could. I felt the tears well up in my eyes, as my hands shook. "Oh, Collin," I exhale.

"Luna?" My mom spoke quietly. I turned around to find her standing behind me.

"Mom," I cried. I collapsed into her arms, sobbing uncontrollably.

"It's okay sweetie, it'll be okay," she comforted me, rubbing her hand across my back.

"No, it won't," I cried into her shoulder. "I've lost him."

"No, you haven't. You can't lose anyone who loves you," she sighed. She pulled away and leads me toward the passenger side of the car, opening the door and helping me inside.

My mom started the car and pulled away from the dorm, heading across campus and back toward home.

I awoke to my mom nudging my shoulder. "We're home, honey," she announced. I slowly crawled out of the car and grabbed my bags out of the backseat. Following my mom inside, and we ordered pizza for dinner.

Still exhausted, I headed to my room to go to sleep. I walked into my room and stop in my tracks, staring at my bed. Damn it. I can't even go to bed without thinking of Eric. He's everywhere.

I climbed under the sheets and pulled my comforter up over my bed, shutting out the world.

I spent the next two days packing every belonging I had to my name. I felt as though I was permanently moving to London with the amount of luggage I had. Luckily, the flight was taken care of through the scholarship committee, so I only had to pay for my boxes I would ship.

On my last night, I decided to send Eric a text message.

"Hey. I'm back in New York for the night
and I wanted to see if you were okay.
Call me."

Send.

I awoke early the next morning before sunrise. As my alarm rang out, I quickly checked to see if I had a missed call.

Nothing. I tossed my phone onto my nightstand and crossed my arms over my face. Great.

I crawled out of bed and hopped into the shower, getting myself ready for the day. I blew out my cherry red hair and painted on some natural makeup before heading out to the kitchen. My mom greeted me with a cup of coffee and a cinnamon bagel. "Good morning," she sang out.

"Good morning," I groaned.

"You about ready to head to the airport?" She asked. I nodded in response and downed my drink before I followed her out the front door.

My mom had rented a small moving truck to transport all of my boxes and bags to the airport. I hopped into the passenger seat as the engine roared alive, making our way out of the driveway.

I gazed out at the stars shining over head as we pulled out onto the open road. For the first time last night, I didn't have my nightmare. I was ready. I was ready to go to London.

Chapter 16

I rode down an escalator from the flight gate to baggage claim. A middle-aged woman in a navy pantsuit was waiting, her dirty blonde hair pulled back tightly in an invisible claw clip. She held up a white sign that read my name, "Luna".

"Hello, Luna. My name is Stacy. I work for the London Scholarship Committee. I'll be escorting you to your new apartment to help get you settled," she greeted me brightly.

"Hi, I'm Luna." I announced awkwardly. "But you already knew that." I chuckled awkwardly, pointing at her sign.

I grabbed my boxes and bags off of the baggage claim conveyer belt, filling up two full carts. A nearby airport attendant helped push one of the carts out toward the taxi curb while I followed behind with the other cart.

Two black town cars waited at the curb, with two thirty-year-old men in a black suits standing by them, prepared to help load my luggage into the two cars.

"Hello ma'am," they greeted me formally. I gave them a nod and hopped into the backseat of the first car with Stacy.

Once, they finished loading my luggage, one of the men climbed into the driver's seat and pulled the car out from the airport, with the other car following behind us.

"This is all very fancy," I exclaimed.

"We want to make sure our candidate is well cared for," Stacy explained. "Now, this is your class schedule, and the buildings they are in. And this is your apartment's address, and the date and time you have a meeting with your guidance counselor," She stated, handing me a handful of documents.

I took the forms from her reluctantly, beginning to feel overwhelmed. "Classes start tomorrow at eight in the morning, giving you today to get settled in. Here is a map of the city with a list of recommended restaurants and coffee shops," she continued on, handing me more documents.

We came to a stop in front of a large stone building with black siding and the name hanging above the front doors. It was a massive building that seemed to go on forever. I followed Stacy out of the car and into the apartment building, as the two men removed my luggage from the cars.

We stepped into an elevator and rode it up to the top floor. Stacy was yammering about the history and architecture of the building, but I couldn't hear a word she was saying. My stomach filled with butterflies, and my ears rang, and I felt as if I could throw up any second.

We stepped off the elevator and made our way down the hall until we stopped at my front door. "Would you like to do the honors?" Stacy asked, holding up a pair of keys. I gently took them from her hand and unlocked the door, stepping inside. The light wood floors and cream white walls made the space feel very open and light.

The furniture and kitchen were all very modern and updated. It was the most expensive looking home I'd ever seen. I walked through the living room and peered into the bedroom. There was a large brown accent wall and white, floor to ceiling closets that stretched along another wall. I walked over to the window and looked outside. We must've been ten stories up. The building continued on and wrapped in a circular shape. It was very modern architecture.

I came back out to the living room and walked over to the balcony. I opened the sliding glass door and stepped out onto the cement ledge. The view was breathtaking. The skyline was endless, infinite, blue. *How beautiful,* I thought.

I stepped back inside the living room to find Stacy directing the two men who unloaded my boxes.

"Well, this is everything," Stacy announced, gesturing to the boxes. "We'll leave you to get settled. And here's my card, if you need anything," she said, handing me her business card. I gave her a nod and they exited from the apartment.

I tossed my keys onto the wooden coffee table and collapsed onto the green fabric sofa. It was much more comfortable than it looked. I scanned the room and let out a deep sigh. *I live here,* I thought. *I actually live here.*

I spent the day unloading box by box and putting away all of my belongings, hanging up my decorations and setting up my closet.

By dinnertime, I was absolutely exhausted. I ordered a greasy cheeseburger from a nearby pub and had it delivered. I didn't have enough energy to go explore tonight.

I climbed into bed and pulled the covers up to my chin. The apartment was pitch black with a small stream of moonlight shining through my curtains. It was deadly silent. The only sound that filled the place was a clock ticking in the living room. I'd never lived on my own before.

It suddenly became lonely, and almost frightening. I decided to turn on a peaceful piano melody to help me sleep and fill the silence in my room.

I awoke the following morning to my alarm ringing in my ear. I quickly shut it off and blinked through the stream of sunlight shining through my curtains. *Here we go,* I thought to myself. I made sure to get up a half an hour early to give myself extra time to ensure I arrived to class early.

I headed into the bathroom to take a shower. Beige stone filled the bathroom from floor to ceiling, contrasting a black tile vanity sink. Fancy. I fumbled with the European shower controls before figuring out how to turn on the hot water.

Once I was ready, I grabbed my backpack and my documents that Stacy gave me and headed out the door.

I made my way down the elevator and out the front door. Traffic rushed past me on the busy street. Car horns filled the air with the smell of fuel exhaust filled my nose. A red double decker bus zoomed by, I stared at it in awe. *Wow, I'm really in London,* I thought. I pinched my forearm, making sure everything was real.

I looked down at my papers for the directions to my first class. I looked to my left and right, trying to find the right street to head out on. But none of the street signs aligned with the directions. Shit. I could feel the heat rising in my cheeks as my hands began to shake. Screw it, we're going to the left.

I made my way down the street, from the left of my apartment, walking quickly so I wouldn't be late for my first class. I walked three blocks down before I stopped in my tracks. *I don't think this is right,* I thought. Ugh. I turned around and fast paced my way back toward my apartment building, I felt myself breaking into a sweat.

I arrived back at my apartment and kept walking, to the right of the building. I walked another block before finally finding the correct street listed in my directions.

"Finally." I exhaled.

I followed the directions to the first building of my classes. It was a large brick building with arched, stone doorways. I took a deep breath before I headed inside the front entrance. I paced down the halls, feeling increasingly worried I was late, since I was the only one out in the hallway.

I ran up the stairs to the second story and found my lecture hall. I opened the door slowly and snuck inside. The professor had already begun their lecture as I scanned the room for a seat. There was an empty seat next to a curly, red headed girl. I shuffled quickly over to her table and took the empty seat. She turned toward me and gave me a soft but warm smile.

I pulled out my laptop and took notes, I felt the sweat beads trickling down my forehead.

As class came to an end, I packed my belongings, getting ready to head back outside.

"Hey, I'm Molly, by the way," The red headed girl greeted me, her British accent rolling richly off her tongue.

"Oh, hey, I'm Luna." I replied shyly. "Sorry if I startled you earlier when I came in. I was running late, obviously."

"Oh, hey, no worries. I barely made it on time myself." Molly chuckled. "So, you sound American. Are you from the States?"

"I am," I confessed as we exited the classroom together. "I've lived in just about half of the fifty states, but right now, my mom and I live in New York"

"No way. That's so cool. I've never been anywhere," Molly explained excitedly. "It must be so nice to travel and explore new places."

"True, but I'm sure it's also nice to have roots planted in one place," I countered.

"You're not wrong there," she agreed. "Hey, do you want to grab some coffee?"

"Sure, why not?" I replied.

Molly took me to the Royal Albert Hall Café Bar for an amazing cup of coffee.

"So are you from London?" I asked Molly as we took a seat at a table.

"No, my family is from Surrey. My three younger sisters still live there, but my two older brothers live here in London for their jobs," she explained.

"Wow, you have a big family." I exclaim."

Molly nodded her head as she took a sip of her coffee. "Yeah, it's not a very quiet home," she laughed. "How about you? Do you have any siblings?"

"No, it's just me and my mom," I explained.

"Must be nice to just have the two of you. I have to commute from home to class every day and not only is the journey over a half an hour, but my house is just chaos," Molly sighed.

"Well, hey, would you want to come back to my apartment after our classes? We can try out and find the best restaurants," I suggested.

"Oh my gosh, yes, that would be awesome!" She smiled

We exchanged phone numbers and continued making small talk until I had to leave for my next class. But not before I confirmed with Molly the right way to get there. It looked like making friends was getting a bit easier.

Molly came over for dinner that night, and we ended up ordering takeout from five of the closest restaurants. We spent the evening laughing and bonding over boys. I told her all about Eric and Collin and she told me about her ex-boyfriend who had recently broken up with her. As it turned out, we were both introverts who struggled communicating with others.

"You should meet my roommate Kaitlin; she can befriend anyone in a room," I announced.

"You should invite her to come to London for the weekend," Molly suggested.

I paused for a moment debating the reality of the suggestion. "You know what, I should. Let's FaceTime her right now!" I exclaimed. I reached for my phone and dialed her number. Kaitlin answered and I introduced her to Molly and asked her to come to London.

"Oh my gosh, yes! That would be so much fun!" Kaitlin cheered. "I'll book my ticket right now." She hung up the phone, and Molly and I let out a squeals with laughter. It looked like London might be fun after all.

Chapter 17

The first week of classes passed by in a blur. I counted down the days until Kaitlin arrived from the states.

On Saturday afternoon, Molly and I took a cab to pick her up from the airport. We waited at baggage claim, staring eagerly at the escalator for her to arrive.

"There she is!" I shouted. Kaitlin trotted down the escalator with her blonde hair in a loose, side braid that laid on her blue jean jacket. She ran toward me screaming and her arms open wide. I returned her embrace and hugged her tightly, a smile stretching widely across my face.

"Kaitlin, this is Molly, Molly this is Kaitlin!" I introduced the two. They smiled and hugged excitedly.

"It's so nice to finally meet you," Kaitlin greeted her.

We grabbed Kaitlin's suitcase and headed out to grab a cab back to the apartment.

"Do you guys want to grab some lunch?" Molly asked.

"Sounds good to me," I replied.

We stopped by my apartment to help Kaitlin settle in before heading to Bill's Baker Street Restaurant. The atmosphere was busy and loud, so we snagged a table on their outside patio.

"Can I start you ladies off with something to drink?" our waiter asked. He was very handsome, a tall, fit blonde with shaggy hair and bright blue eyes.

Once we placed our orders, Kaitlin turned to me with an intrigued expression. "So, have you heard from Eric?" she asked. My heart dropped.

"Oh, Eric, he's the ex, right?" Molly questioned. Kaitlin nodded to her in confirmation.

"Uh, no." I hesitated. "I don't imagine that I will. I hurt him pretty badly when I told him I wouldn't go to Colorado with him." I tugged at a hole in my black jeans.

"Makes sense, I guess. Although you two were so close, I can't imagine you'll never hear from him again." Kaitlin comforted me. Molly nodded in agreement.

"I don't know you guys. I've reached out several times and he still hasn't responded. I think it's over for good," I explained.

"What about that Collin guy?" Molly asked. "Have you heard from him either?"

"Nope." I shook my head. "All the boys are gone." I laughed nervously, suddenly feeling very lonely.

"Well, hey that's not a bad thing! I mean, hello! You're in London! This is the perfect time to meet someone new! Have a spontaneous summer love in a foreign country. I mean, that's the literal dream," Kaitlin encouraged me.

Before I could respond, our waiter arrived back at the table with our food. As he set our plates down, Kaitlin gave Molly a mischievous look.

"Hey, I'm Kaitlin." She extended her hand to our waiter.

"Hey, I'm Edward," he greeted her, his rich English accent filling the air.

"This is my friend, Luna," she replied, gesturing toward me. "She just moved here and needs some fun. Do you know of any good hangout spots?" she questioned him.

"Well, there's a dance club just a few blocks south from here, if you girls are interested." He smiled.

"Oh my gosh, a club is perfect!" Molly chimed in.

"Absolutely, pick us up at nine?" Kaitlin nudged Edward.

"Can't wait. I'll see you guys tonight." He smiled.

"Oh my gosh, you guys I cannot believe you just did that," I whispered as Edward left the table.

"Oh, come on babe. Live a little," Kaitlin teased me.

"We've got to go shopping for tonight!" Molly exclaimed. She and Kaitlin cheered in unison as we began to eat our food.

After lunch we decided to head into the heart of London and spend the rest of the afternoon shopping. Kaitlin settled on a red, cocktail dress with matching red heels. Whereas Molly purchased a short, emerald, green dress with nude heels, and I bought a little black dress with matching black heels. Kaitlin must be rubbing off on me, because I put up little argument against my outfit that she and Molly had chosen for me.

We headed back to my apartment to get ready. I hopped in the shower as Molly and Kaitlin gave each other manicures and pedicures. Once I blew my hair out, Kaitlin curled my cherry-colored hair into loose beach waves as Molly painted on my makeup. She gave me a very dramatic appearance with gold glitter eye shadow and a cat eye with black liquid eyeliner.

Kaitlin curled Molly's hair as well as I painted on her makeup. We laughed and gossiped about Edward as we got ready. I'd never gone to homecoming or prom. This must be what those nights felt like with your girlfriends. It was nice. I could get used to this.

My apartment buzzer beeped right at 9 o'clock. My heart skipped a beat.

"He's here!" Kaitlin shrieked. We grabbed our purses and headed out the door as my hands shook.

We walked out the front entrance of the building and found Eric waiting on the sidewalk with a cab ready. His blonde hair perfectly styled, and he wore a navy suit with brown dress shoes.

"Hey Edward!" Kaitlin greeted him with a friendly hug. "You remember Luna," she smiled, pulling me toward him. We climbed into the cab and headed off toward the club.

"So, Edward, Luna has moved to England for the summer for an art scholarship," Kaitlin announced.

"No kidding. That's amazing." He smiled at me.

"Yeah, it's pretty cool," I chuckled nervously. *God why am I so awkward?* I thought to myself.

We arrived at the club and Edward gave me his hand, helping me out of the car. There was a long line roped off out front of the building with a bouncer standing guard. Edward approached the bouncer and said something to him out of ear shot. The bouncer lifted a clipboard he held, examining it for a moment before stepping to the side, unhooking a red rope and letting us in.

The music was pounding, flashing neon lights filled the room, and a massive crowd danced on the dance floor.

"Let's go get a drink!" Kaitlin shouted over the music. We each nodded in agreement and headed over to the bar. Edward ordered us a round and we found a place to stand.

"Let's go dance!" Molly suggested. Kaitlin nodded, and Edward and I followed them out to the middle of the dance floor. We formed a circle and danced to the beat. I laughed and smiled with Kaitlin and Molly as they spun me around, swaying our hips to the beat of the music. We danced to a few songs together before Molly whispered to Kaitlin, pointing across the room at two guys.

"We're going to go talk to them!" they announced. Before I could protest, they ran away, leaving me alone with Edward. I was so embarrassed.

"We can go with them if you want." Edward suggested, sensing my nerves.

I glanced over at Molly and Kaitlin laughing with their guys and looked back to Edward. I shook my head and set my drink down at a nearby table before wrapping my arms around his neck.

"I'd rather dance with you," I shouted over the music.

"Me, too." He smiled down at me, placing his hands on my waist.

We danced the night away, laughing and making small talk over the music until the bartenders turned the club's lights on, announcing last call. We met back up with Molly and Kaitlin and headed outside to catch a cab.

Edward stood behind me out on the curb with his arms wrapped around me. We swayed slowly back and forth as we waited for our cab to arrive. I couldn't remember the last time I'd felt this comfortable.

As the cab pulled up on the street, Edward opened the door for Kaitlin and Molly to climb inside the car and followed inside after me. We held hands the entire car ride back to my place, listening to Kaitlin and Molly gush over the two new guys they'd met.

I rested my head on his shoulder, feeling the exhaustion begin to set in. This was nice.

We arrived back at my apartment, and all tumbled out of the cab. Molly and Kaitlin said their goodbyes to Edward and then headed inside to give us some privacy.

"I had a really nice time tonight." He turned toward me.

"Me too." I smiled up at him. He reached up slowly, brushing a hair behind my ear before leaning in and gently kissing my cheek. I felt butterflies fill my stomach as my hands shook.

"Goodnight, Luna," he whispered in my ear before climbing back into the cab and driving off into the night.

Chapter 18

We spent the next two days touring the famous sites of London: the London Eye, Westminster Abbey, Tower of London, Buckingham Palace, and so much more. My feet had never been sorer. But my heart was so full. Kaitlin made sure to take a selfie with Molly and I at every location to mark the occasion. Her inner photographer shone.

By Monday morning, I felt I knew London better than New York back home. Come to think of it, I never went anywhere other than school and home. I knew absolutely nothing about the part of New York where I lived. Oh well.

Molly came over to the apartment to take Kaitlin to the airport with me.

"I can't believe you already have to go. It feels like you just got here," Molly whined.

"I know. To be honest, I wish I didn't have to leave. It's been so much fun staying here with you guys," Kaitlin admitted. I gave her a big hug, suddenly feeling melancholy about her soon-to-be absence.

"So why don't you stay for the summer? I have an extra futon. We could all live together here in Luna's fancy apartment," Molly suggested. I gave Molly a sympathetic smile. Before glancing over to Kaitlin.

"You know what? Why don't you stay for the summer?" I asked Kaitlin. Kaitlin let out a dramatic laugh. "Oh, come on you guys, there's no ways," she laughed.

"Why not?" Molly questioned. "You said it yourself; you'll just be moping around at home. Come stay here with us. The three of us would have so much fun living together!"

Kaitlin glanced to me, beginning to seriously ponder the idea. We stood in silence.

"Okay." Kaitlin smiled. Molly jumped up shrieking, Kaitlin joining in. They each grabbed me by the arm and pulled me into a group hug.

"This is going to be the best summer ever!" Molly cheered. We all tumbled to the floor, laughing in unison.

"Okay, well, first things first. We have to get you home so you can pack!" I exclaimed. I grabbed Kaitlin's suitcase, and we headed out the apartment door.

We caught a cab and dropped Kaitlin off at the airport, giving her endless hugs.

"I'll see you guys in just a few days!" Kaitlin smiled. We could barely contain our excitement. She boarded her plane and Molly, and I headed back out to the taxi lane, arm in arm.

Molly climbed into a cab to head back home and get ready for class, whereas I grabbed my own separate cab to head home. I smiled like an uncontrollable idiot the entire car ride back to my apartment.

As my car pulled up the curb to park, I noticed a blond man standing outside the front entrance of my building. He held a bouquet of yellow lilies. *Oh, my God, it's Edward.* I climbed out of the car and slowly walked toward him, feeling my heart pounding in my chest.

"Hey, I was hoping to catch you." He smiled. I glanced at the flowers in his hands. "Oh, these are for you," he stated handing them to me.

"Wow, thank you. This is too much." I smiled shyly.

"Well, I saw them and thought of you," he said coolly. "So, I had fun the other night."

"So did I," I replied awkwardly.

"I'd love to take you out some time. Maybe this Friday?" he asked. I looked down at the flowers in hand, feeling my heart skip a beat.

"Yeah, that sounds nice." I smiled. *He could be the summer romance I need,* I thought to myself. *He could help me finally get over Eric.*

He leaned in slowly and kissed my cheek gently, goose bumps raising at the touch of his lips.

"I'll see you soon," he whispered and gave me a devilish wink before heading down the sidewalk. I gazed after him, smiling, feeling truly happy.

I spent the rest of the day in a haze. I walked from class to class, daydreaming of my date with Edward. Where would we go? What would we do? What would he want to talk about? Oh, God, what would I say?

I felt my nerves set in. My phone dinged and pulled me out of my head. I reached for it and saw it was a text message from Eric. My heart dropped.

"Hey. I hope you're enjoying London.
I miss you."

Oh, my God, he texted me. He actually texted me. What do I say back?

"Hey. London is amazing. I miss you, too" Send. Short, sweet, and to the point.

I spent the rest of the evening attempting to study, but I failed. I couldn't focus if my life depended on it. I would check my phone every thirty seconds only to be disappointed. He hadn't texted me back.

By Wednesday morning, I was relieved to be heading back to the airport to pick up Kaitlin. Molly met me out front of my apartment to ride there together.

We greeted her with open arms at baggage claim as we waited for her suitcases. Molly asked her how her flight was when someone caught the corner of my eye. It was Collin. I caught his eye as we stared at each other stunned. Kaitlin followed my gaze, seeing Collin across the room with his family.

"Oh, my God," She whispered to me. She gave him a friendly wave, and he awkwardly shuffled toward us.

"Hey," he greeted us shyly.

"Hey, what're you doing here?" Kaitlin greeted him with a hug.

"My dad's old business partner just moved out here a few months ago, and he invited us to come stay for a few weeks," he explained. I nodded in understanding as Collin turned toward me. "I'm sorry. I should've texted you to let you know, but I figured what were the odds of us actually running into each other?" He laughed. "I guess very high."

We stood awkwardly together, unable to find words to fill the air when Kaitlin finally broke the silence.

"Well, hey, you should come and get coffee with us sometime while you're here," she suggested. Collin looked at me for permission.

"Oh, yeah, there's a great coffee shop by my apartment. You should come," I agreed.

"That sounds great," he exclaimed with a half-smile.

We said our goodbyes and headed out of the airport to go back to my apartment. I glanced back at Collin as he walked back toward his family. Maybe this could be a new beginning for us.

Chapter 19

"Oh, my god- I can't believe we just ran into Collin!" Kaitlin exclaimed as we walked inside my apartment.

"I know, how weird is that?" I replied, still in shock.

"Remind me who Collin is?" Molly asked.

"Oh, he's the one who confessed his feelings for Luna right before she came here." Kaitlin explained.

"Oh, yeah that's right. He was hot! Why didn't you go for him?" Molly teased.

"Because she's still in love with Eric," Kaitlin mocked me.

"Geez, Luna, what's your secret to getting all these guys to fall for you?" Molly laughed.

"Ha, ha, very funny." I replied sarcastically.

"No, seriously, I've never had a boyfriend. Guys never go for me. What do you do to get them to like you?" Molly asked.

I paused for a moment, contemplating my answer. "Honestly, nothing," I confessed.

"Damn, I was hoping for a little more," Molly whined. We went into my bedroom and pushed my bed over a few feet to set up Molly's futon for Kaitlin.

"I cleared some space in my dresser and bathroom for you." I explained to her.

"Oh, thanks!" Kaitlin smiled. Molly and I went back into the living room to help unpack the rest of Kaitlin's bags.

We spent a few hours helping to get Kaitlin settled in before Molly and I had to go to class. I felt very whole having Kaitlin here. It was like being back in the dorm only better, because now I had Molly, too. I'd never had a best friend before I met Kaitlin and now, I had two. How did I get to be so lucky?

That night, we decided to go out to dinner at Circolo Popolare to celebrate Kaitlin's moving in. The restaurant was busy, but the food was incredible.

"Hey, Molly, do you want to crash at our place tonight?" Kaitlin asks.

"Yeah! Then we can walk to class together tomorrow morning, Luna." Molly replied, excitedly.

"I think my couch has a pull-out bead that you can sleep on." I offered, sipping on my soda.

"Sounds great!" Molly smiled. Just then, my phone dinged with a text message. It was from Collin.

"Hey, can we meet for coffee tomorrow morning?"

I showed the message to the girls, wondering what to reply.

"Um is that even a question? Of course you should go, talk to him. Clear the air between you two!" Kaitlin encouraged me. I nodded in agreement.

'Hey, that sounds great, 8 a.m.?' Send.

We paid the bill and headed back home. Settling in for the night, Molly and I worked on our homework together on the couch, while Kaitlin continued to unpack.

I got up early the following morning to meet Collin. "Wish me luck!" I called out, heading for the door.

"Good luck!" Kaitlin and Molly cheered in unison.

I headed out for the coffee shop, feeling my heartbeat in my ears as my hands shook. I tried to contain my nerves but found it increasingly difficult to hide.

I arrived at the restaurant to find Collin waiting by the front entrance. "Hey." I greeted him nervously.

"Hey, thanks for meeting me." Collin smiled, and I could tell he was nervous too. What a relief.

We headed inside and found a booth in the back corner, sipping on our coffee quietly, both trying to find the courage to start a conversation.

"So, I'm glad you reached out," I started, trying to break the ice.

"Oh, yeah, well, I know things have been awkward between us, and that's partially my fault but I'd still like to be friends if that's possible." Collin replies.

"Of course we can still be friends Collin." I encouraged, reaching for his hand. "I've really enjoyed our friendship this past year, and I'd really love it if we could go back to that."

"Yeah, that sounds nice. I mean, I don't know if it would be the same, but I think starting over is a good idea," he explained. I nodded in agreement. "I'm also sorry I didn't message you that I was coming to London. As I mentioned, before I thought about it, but chickened out."

"Hey, no worries, I would've chickened out too," I comforted him.

We spent the next hour catching up on life. Collin explained about an internship he was looking into applying for, this fall. And how his family had been driving him crazy since he moved back home for the summer.

"Well, I should probably get going to class," I announced. We paid the bill and headed outside. Collin walked with me across campus to the building my class was in. We arrived to find Molly waiting for me outside the front entrance.

"Hey! You made it just in time," she greeted us.

"Yeah... uh, Collin this is my good friend, Molly, Molly, this is Collin from back home." I introduced them.

"Hey, it's great to meet you." Collin smiled, extending out a hand to Molly.

"Hi," Molly's face turned bright red as she shook Collin's hand. She ran a shaky finger through her curly, auburn hair.

"Luna was just telling me how you two met. It's nice she has such a good friend here in London," Collin winked. Molly looked down at her shoes, trying to hide her rosy cheeks.

"Hopefully, she's only said good things." Molly smiled.

"Very good things," Collin smirked. They gazed into each other's eyes for a moment, forgetting my presence.

"Okay, well, we should probably get to class," I announced, startling them both of them.

"Oh, yeah, we probably should," Molly hesitated, still staring into Collin's eyes.

"All right, well, let's get together again before you leave," I said to Collin.

"Yeah, that sounds great." We gave each other a quick hug before Collin turned back to Molly.

"I guess I'll see you later." He smiled at her.

"Yeah, uh, that'd be nice," she choked.

"I look forward to it." He winked at her, giving his devilish smile before he hailed a cab and headed back to his family.

I gave Molly a smirk and linked my arm with hers, dragging her inside the building to head to class.

"Oh, my God!" Molly cried out. "Did you see that! He was flirting with me! A boy- a real boy- was flirting with me, and not just any boy, but a really hot boy!"

"I'm really happy for you, Molly," I exclaimed, but I couldn't fight the slight nagging sensation in my gut.

As we walked to class together, Molly was in a complete daz; she didn't take a single note the entire lecture. Oh boy.

Chapter 20

I awoke to my phone dinging in my ear. I rolled over in bed to find a text message from Edward:

"Are you free this afternoon?"

I rolled back onto my side and glanced over at Kaitlin, who was softly snoring on her futon next to me. I paused for a moment, pondering my answer before finally responding:

"Where should I meet you?" Send.

"How about at the Diana Princess of Wales Memorial Fountain? 5 p.m.?"

"Can't wait. See you soon." Send.

Well, it looked like I was going on a date. I gulped. I set my phone down and let out a deep exhale. *What should I wear?* I thought. *Should I curl my hair? Or maybe wear it in a bun? Should I wear sandals? Damnit, what did I get myself into?*

"Hey," Kaitlin whispered to me. I turned over to see that she was awake. "You, okay?"

"Oh, yeah, I'm fine." My stress must've woken her. "Go back to sleep." She shook her head and stretched her arms out.

"Nah, I'm up for the day. Coffee?" She asked. I nodded in agreement. We each climbed out of our beds and headed into the living room. Molly was spread out on the pull-out sofa bed, scrolling through her phone.

"Good morning," she greeted us.

"Morning," we replied in unison. Molly had practically moved in after Kaitlin did, spending more nights with us than she did at her own home.

The three of us sat down at the kitchen table, sipping on our coffees and eating muffins for breakfast.

"So, this just happened," I announced, passing them my phone.

"Ooh yes, girl! My Luna has a date!" Kaitlin cheered.

"Relax- it's nothing serious, super casual," I explained, trying to convince myself more than them.

Kaitlin and Molly grinned at the idea and teased me before I decided it was time to get ready for class.

Classes passed by in a blur. All I could focus on was Edward and our date. I hardly took any notes on the lectures and ended up having to borrow from Molly.

Molly and I got back to the apartment that afternoon, and she and Kaitlin immediately started dressing me up.

"Okay, so I got this dress out of my closet that I thought would look so pretty on you." Kaitlin smiled, holding up an emerald- green dress. It was sleeveless with a sweetheart neckline and spaghetti straps. The top half of the dress fit like a glove whereas the bottom half was loose and flowing. It was perfect.

Molly painted on my makeup as Kaitlin curled my hair into loose beach waves. Both of them were more excited about this date than I was. I could feel my hands begin to shake as my heart started to race.

"I don't know if I can do this." I choke.

"Oh, Luna yes you can. You can do this. You'll go, talk, walk, smile, maybe even have a good time." Kaitlin encouraged.

"Yeah, I mean just remember how much fun that night was with him at the club. You two enjoy each other's company and like spending time together. Just have some fun," Molly chimed in.

"Okay, well, when you put it like that, I guess it doesn't seem so scary." I admitted. They both smiled at me in unison.

"You've got this." Kaitlin nudged me. "Okay, you're all ready!"

I walked into the bathroom and gazed at myself in the mirror.

"Wow." I exhaled. "You guys are magicians." I smiled.

"Oh, stop, you're gorgeous, Luna. We just accentuated it." Kaitlin winked.

I took a deep breath and headed out the door, feeling like butterflies were filling my gut.

I caught a cab and headed to the fountain. I was excited to see the monument. I could feel a small smile spread across my cheeks the closer we got to the destination.

The cab pulled up to the fountain and I climbed out of it, thanking the driver. It was beautiful. There was hardly anyone there, and the sun was shining in a bright blue sky. The fountain flooded to life with water shooting out in each direction. The view was breath taking.

"You look amazing," a familiar voice announced. I turned around to find Edward walking toward me with a picnic basket in hand. He stepped forward and placed the basket on the ground before wrapping his arms around my waist and pulling me in for a hug.

"I'm so glad you came." He smiled.

"Me too." I smiled back. "Thank you for setting this up."

"Of course. Shall we?" He gestures toward the fountain. I nodded in response and followed along beside him hand in hand.

We found an open spot on the grass, and Edward pulled out a blanket from the basket, laying it on the ground for us to sit on. We took a seat before he revealed the remaining contents inside the basket. He pulled out a bottle of wine, sandwiches, grapes, and chocolate covered strawberries.

"Oh my gosh, this all looks amazing." I gasped. "Thank you for putting all of this together," I said as I reached for a grape.

"It was my pleasure." His British accent rolled off his tongue as he opened the bottle of wine.

"So, tell me, how do you like London so far?" He asked.

"Oh my gosh, it's been amazing. My roommates and I went site seeing, and we've tried out a ton of different restaurants, and school has been incredible. I feel like I'm learning so much more here than at school in Rhode Island. But then again, I've only been there for one semester," I laughed.

"I'm glad to hear it's going so well. And I love your American accent. It's so refreshing and beautiful." He smiled. "Maybe we can do some sight-seeing ourselves sometime."

"Yeah, that would be great," I smiled back. We spent the next hour talking, eating, and laughing. Molly was right. Edward and I got along really well. Maybe this could be the summer romance I needed. The thought was encouraging for a moment before I felt an ache in my gut.

Edward leaned forward and brushed my hair behind my ear before leaning in all the way and pressing his lips against mine. I kissed him back passionately, craving him. But something inside me made me stop. I pulled away from him quickly, abruptly stopping our moment.

"Is everything okay?" he asked concerned.

"Oh, yeah, everything is fine, it's just..." I began to choke on my own words. "I'm not sure I can do this." I looked down at my hands, fidgeting with my fingers. Edward reached out his hand and intertwined his fingers with mine.

"Hey, that's okay. We can take it slow if you want," he offered. I looked deep into his bright blue eyes, there was a sense of calm and genuine reassurance there.

"You are extremely kind, Edward," I admitted. "But I can't lead you on. It wouldn't be fair."

He pulled his hand back from mine.

"You mean, you don't want to be together at all?" He questioned.

"No, I do! Of course I do." I admitted. "It's just I'm still getting over a breakup and I'm not quite over it yet, and I wouldn't be able to give you all that you deserve."

He dropped his head and lets out a deep exhale.

"Yeah, okay, I understand," he breathed.

"You have no idea, how badly I wanted this to work. I really thought this could be an amazing summer romance," I exhaled.

"Yeah, me, too," he admitted. "Well, I guess we'd better head home then," he stated as he began packing up the picnic. I helped him put everything back in the basket before we stood up and walked toward the street.

Edward hailed me a cab and opened the door to help me inside. Just as I was climbing into the cab, I stopped and turned to him. "Thank you for a lovely picnic, I'm so sorry it had to end like this." I leaned forward and kissed him on the cheek before climbing all the way into the car.

Chapter 21

"Hey, we should invite Collin over before he heads back to the States," Kaitlin suggested.

"Yeah, that's a good idea. I'll shoot him a text," I agreed. I've been in a funk the last few weeks since my date with Edward. I felt incredibly guilty about leading him on but sad that I ended things between us. *Why does love have to be so complicated?* I thought to myself.

I sent Collin a text about coming over to the apartment, and he agreed and decided to come over for lunch.

Kaitlin, Molly, and I spent our morning cleaning the apartment for his arrival. I think it's the first time I'd cleaned since I'd lived here. Not that the place was overly dirty. Kaitlin was always tidying up, being the neat freak she was.

I hopped in the shower and got myself ready, settling on a black tank top with jean shorts. I blow-dried my hair and put on some light, natural makeup.

The doorbell rang and I ran to buzz Collin in.

"Come on up!" I cheered. Collin knocked at the door a moment later and I walked over the door to let him.

"Hey, how are you?" I greeted him.

"I'm good. Thanks for having me over." He smiled. He was wearing a navy V-neck T-shirt with cargo shorts and grey sneakers.

Collin stepped inside the living room and immediately locked eyes with Molly. "Hey, Molly... How are you?" He greeted her with a wink.

"Oh, uh, I'm good," she choked, turning bright red like her auburn hair.

"Would you like some coffee?" I offered.

"Yeah, that would be great." He smiled.

I headed into the kitchen and put on a pot of coffee.

"So are you guys getting ready for fall semester? It's just a few weeks away." Collin asked.

"Yeah, I was just looking over my class schedule for this year, I'm dreading my 8 a.m. class." Kaitlin chimed in.

I glanced at Molly who had a saddened expression.

"I can't imagine leaving this place," I announced. "I've gotten so used to living here with you two that it's hard to think of leaving."

"Yeah, I hate to think of you guys leaving," Molly admitted.

"Me too girl, I can't imagine living without you," Kaitlin comforted her, wrapping her arm around Molly's shoulder.

We all fell silent. The melancholy vibe filled the air.

"Hey, why don't you apply to study abroad at our school?" I suggested.

"Oh, my God, what a great idea! You could come study with us, and we could all live together in a dorm!" Kaitlin cheered.

"Do you really think it's possible?" Molly perked up.

"Yeah, I mean why not? We've probably missed the deadline for fall semester, but you could come for spring semester and stay for the summer! We could all get an apartment together." Kaitlin clapped, jumping up and down.

"Oh my gosh, yes! Let's do it!" Molly cried out, jumping up and down with Kaitlin. I looked over at Collin who had a wide grin on his face.

"Okay, I'm going to go to the study abroad guidance counselor right now and fill out the forms!" Molly announced, grabbing her bag.

"I'll come with you- that way I can give them all the info you need for the school." Kaitlin encourages.

They grabbed their belongings and headed out the door. They shut the door behind them, leaving Collin and me to ourselves.

"Looks like we'll have a fourth person for our coffee dates," I teased him.

"I know. I can't wait." He smiled. I arched my brow giving him a teasing expression.

"What? Oh come on, don't look at me like that," he chuckled.

"Okay, okay." I laughed. "You want some lunch? I know a great sandwich place we could get carryout from."

"Sounds great," he agreed.

I grabbed my phone, pulling up the restaurant website and we placed our orders.

We spent the next hour chatting and eating our lunch, hanging out until Molly and Kaitlin arrived back from the administration office.

"We're back!" They announced as they came in through the front door.

"Hey! How'd it go?" I asked.

"Well, I got all of the forms filled out and submitted, so now we wait. They said it will probably be about two weeks or so before I hear anything." Molly explained.

"I hate that we have to wait that long to find out. I want to start planning now," Kaitlin sighed.

"We can still plan; besides, we'll have to have a meeting with the housing department. Once we get back to request our room and board with her once she arrives." I explained.

"Oh, you're right. Good thinking." Kaitlin agreed.

"Yeah, and I would do that sooner rather than later to guarantee you guys will get the room you want." Collin chimed in. We each nodded in unison.

"I should start a list and write all of this down," Kaitlin announced. She grabbed a pad and pen and pulled up a chair next to me at the kitchen table.

We spent the rest of the afternoon making plans and getting everything sorted and organized. Kaitlin and Molly began planning the color schemes or our new room and deciding what decorations to buy.

My heart felt whole. I gave Collin a genuine smile.

"I can't wait for what next year is going to bring." I announced.

Chapter 22

We settled into a routine over the next few weeks. Molly and I walked to class together while Kaitlin walked the local markets and read at the park.

That day, Molly received a text message from her mom that she'd received a large packet in the mail. We both knew what it was for. She left our last class early to head home and to pick it up. But not before she promised not to open the package until she was with us back at the apartment.

I was on pins and needles the rest of the class, wondering what the answer the package would reveal to us.

I hurried home and told Kaitlin about the mail. We sat at the kitchen table, waiting for Molly to arrive.

After a few short moments, the front door swung open and in ran Molly, holding a very thick envelope.

She approached the table and tossed her bag onto the floor, setting the package down in front of us. We each stared at each other for a moment in silence before Molly reached for the envelope, slowly opening it. Kaitlin reached for my hand, gripping it tightly in anticipation.

Molly pulled out a large packet of paper and began reading it, studying it intently. She suddenly broke out in a screaming cheer, jumping up and down. Kaitlin and I jumped up, cheering in unison, reaching out to Molly for a group hug.

"I'm accepted! I'm accepted! I'm coming to live with you guys for spring semester!" Molly cried out.

"I can't believe it! This is so exciting!" Kaitlin cheered.

We stood in a group hug, before pulling away in smiles.

"I'm so happy for you, Molly," I smiled.

"Thanks, Luna. I'm so relieved I don't have to give you guys a final goodbye. It'll just be 'a see you soon goodbye' because I'll be seeing you soon in the spring!" Molly laughed.

"I know. It's going to be so great," Kaitlin chimed in. "We've got to start really planning. I'll call the housing administration and set up an appointment with them for as soon as we get back home next week."

"I can't believe you guys leave in just a week," Molly exclaimed. "I know it's only going to be a few months, but I'm really going to miss seeing you two every day."

"I know, but we'll be able to FaceTime each day, we'll find a good time to talk with our time zones. And we can send post cards and letters. Plus, we have social media, of course. So it'll be like we never really separated." I comforted them.

"Yeah, that's true," Molly said sadly.

"Besides, you're going to be taking classes on designing fashion clothes, so you'll have plenty to send us and to keep you busy." I winked at her.

"Oh, speaking of, let me show you the dress I finally finished making." Molly cheered!

She reached into her backpack and pulled out a long, emerald-green gown. It was beautiful. Covered in intricate detailed lace, it was the most stunning gown I had ever seen.

"I made it for you, Luna. It's your size and color." Molly announced, handing it to me.

"What? Molly, I can't accept this." I said shocked, taking the dress from her.

"Of course you can. You were my first real friend I made at this school, plus you and Kaitlin made me feel so welcomed. So I wanted to make you something special." Molly smiled.

"Molly, this was so sweet of you to do," Kaitlin exclaimed.

"Seriously, Molly, thank you so much, I feel bad I don't have anything to give you in return," I admitted.

"Oh, stop, you don't need to give me anything. Our friendship is more than enough," Molly replied whole heartedly.

"This calls for a bottle of wine to celebrate!" Kaitlin cried out.

"Oh, absolutely!" Molly agreed.

We spent the night ordering take out and drinking wine together. Molly covered the living room floor with different types of fabric for a new fashion project she was working on.

I was working on a painting I was finishing for a class and set up on my easel in the corner. While Kaitlin read her book on the sofa. We talked and laughed through the night, working on our projects and savoring the last few days we had together.

Kaitlin and I spent our last few days in London packing up the apartment. When I wasn't elbow deep in a box with bubble wrap with Kaitlin, I was at the library with my nose in a book with Molly.

Final exams were on the horizon and no amount of studying would relieve my stress. However, it was a good distraction from the melancholy feeling brewing in my gut. I couldn't bear the thought of leaving London. It was my home.

After spending three months there, it felt like I was meant to stay here, even though I had a life waiting for me back in Rhode Island. Not to mention I hadn't seen my mom, either. God, I missed my mom. Living with the girls was a huge help to prevent feeling home sick. But, I prevented myself from thinking of home, afraid of the emotions that would arrive with it.

With one day left, the apartment was filled with boxes. There wasn't any room left for Molly's belongings, forcing her to move back home. However, she was still able to stay the night, leaving room for the pull-out bed on the couch.

One more day to go.

Chapter 23

Kaitlin and I woke up before dawn to prepare for the airport. We rented a moving van to carry all of our boxes and belongings.

"Are you guys ready to go?" Molly asked, handing us each a cup of coffee.

"I think so. The movers should be here at any moment," I announced.

Just as the word escaped my lips, the doorbell buzzed. I headed over to buzz up the movers to our floor.

Three older men came in and started taking our boxes down to the truck.

Once the moving truck was loaded, we caught a cab, and we headed to the airport.

"I can't believe you guys are already leaving," Molly stated.

"I know. I feel like I just moved here," I admitted.

We spent the cab ride reminiscing over the last three months. The site seeing, restaurants we tried, meeting Edward and living together. We made so many memories here. It was hard to leave.

We arrived at the airport and headed over to bag check. Kaitlin and I checked all of our boxes and luggage for our flights. I felt nervous about flying home alone. Part of me wished Kaitlin and I were flying together. However, I was going home to New York, and she was flying home to Ohio.

Luckily, we are only staying home for a few days before moving into our new dorm at school in Rhode Island.

Once our bags were checked, we headed toward security.

"Well, I guess this is where we say goodbye," I announced, turning toward Molly.

"Ugh, this is the moment I've been dreading," Molly choked.

"Oh, honey, come here." Kaitlin comforted Molly. She stretched out her arms and pulled Molly and me in for a big group hug. Molly softly sobbed as we hugged each other goodbye.

"I promise we'll call; we'll FaceTime; we'll write. Spring semester is just a few months away," Kaitlin encouraged her.

"You're right, you're right. Okay, well I guess I'll see you guys soon," Molly sniffled.

We had one more group hug before Kaitlin and I turned to head through security.

Once we got through security, Kaitlin and I said our goodbyes before splitting ways to head to our flight gates.

"Okay well, I'll see you in a few days," Kaitlin announced.

"Yeah, call me and let me know what time you want to meet at the dorm to move in," I asked.

"I will. Don't forget to FaceTime me every day," Kaitlin pleaded.

"I promise." I smiled. We gave each other one last hug before separating ways.

I caught my flight and spent the plane ride sleeping and reading. I didn't realize how truly exhausted I was until I sat down and allowed myself to relax.

When my flight landed, I headed out toward the baggage claim curb, looking for the moving truck my mom was supposed to be picking me up in. I scanned the cars when I heard a car horn. I turned to find my mom pulling up the curb behind me, waving at me ecstatically.

She jumped out of the car and ran to me with open arms.

"My Luna!" She cried out. I ran into her embrace and hugged her back tightly.

"Oh, mom, you have no idea how much I've missed you!" I cried, tears running down my face.

"Oh, honey, I'm so happy you're home. I missed you so much. Come on, let's go home and eat some red velvet cake!" She cheered.

We loaded up the moving van and headed for home. It felt so nice to be back home.

The entire drive home, my mom interrogated me with questions about my stay in London. "Did you have fun? Are you happy or sad to be home? Do you want to go back? How's Molly? Did she cry?" She asked.

"Easy, mom, one question at a time," I laughed.

We arrived home and unloaded the van. It was nice to be back in my old room with my old bed. I collapsed onto my comforter and looked around the room, gazing at all of the boxes that now cluttered my floor.

"Luna! The cake is ready!" My mom called from the kitchen. God, it was so nice to hear her voice.

Chapter 24

I awoke early in the morning, ready to face the day. It was move in day at Kaitlin's and my new dorm. The car was packed, and coffee was brewing in the kitchen.

I took a shower and got myself ready, wearing a gray top with jean shorts and my black Converse.

"Luna, coffee is ready!" My mom called from the kitchen.

I grabbed my last bag and headed out to greet her.

"Good morning," I smiled.

"Good morning, sweetie," she greeted me and handed me a cup of coffee.

I took a large sip and let out a deep sigh- the taste of utter bliss.

"You ready to go?" She asked. I nodded in response and followed her out the door.

We drove for the next several hours, heading back to Rhode Island. My heart ached at the thought of going back to college. I missed London, I missed Molly and Edward. I missed the bustling streets and rainy atmosphere. London was amazing. But Rhode Island was another dream, I just needed to rediscover it.

After several hours, we arrived at my new dorm building. It was half past twelve, and I know Kaitlin had arrived at eight, when the doors opened. She had already moved in and decorated, eager to start this next chapter.

We parked the car in the sea of other families unloading and moving into their nearby buildings. My mom popped the trunk and we each grabbed a box, heading inside the Steven's Building.

We were greeted by the residential assistant, who guided us to my room. This year, the boys and girls were mixed together. Unlike last year, where the girls were on one side of the building with the boys were on the other.

I found our room to find that our next-door neighbors were two boys. *Oh great,* I thought. I opened the door to find Kaitlin sitting at her desk, putting on makeup.

"Luna!" She shouted, rushing toward me with open arms. "I'm so glad you're finally here!"

"Hey, Kaitlin." I smiled. "Sorry we're late. I know you've probably been here for a few hours."

"Hey, no worries. I hope you don't mind I took the top bunk again," she announced.

"No worries, you know I like the bottom bunk." I teased her.

My mom and I set our boxes down and headed back out to the car to collect the rest of my belongings. Kaitlin followed behind, helping to carry the boxes inside.

Once we unloaded the car, we got to work unpacking my things. I started to feel like a nomad, constantly moving from one place to the next, which was ironic, since that was all I'd done my whole life.

Kaitlin set up my art easel in the corner next to the futon and hung up my decorations as I unpacked my clothes, and my mom made my bed. The three of us made a great team.

By dinnertime, we had finished unpacking all of Kaitlin's and my belongings, finally settling into our room.

"You girls must be starving; do you want to grab something to eat? I can order us some pizza?" My mom asked.

"That sounds great!" Kaitlin cheered. I nodded in agreement.

My mom stepped out into the hallway to call the pizza shop, as loud booming music shook our room from upstairs.

"Boy, I did not miss that," I groaned.

"Welcome back to college life," Kaitlin teased me.

"I was spoiled with that nice apartment in London. Only adults lived there, making it a nice, quiet atmosphere," I reminisced.

"I know. That place was super nice, I really miss it, and Molly," Kaitlin admitted. "Have you talked to her yet today?"

"I texted her before we left the house, but she went to bed shortly after. I promised her a FaceTime though tonight once we moved in." I explained.

"So did I," Kaitlin laughed.

"Okay girls, dinner is on the way." My mom announced

"Thanks, mom." I smiled.

The pizza arrived a little while later and the three of us sat on the floor, picnic style. We reminisced about London and told my mom stories about the sites we'd seen. We laughed and talked about Edward and Molly.

"I can't wait to meet Molly in the spring. She sounds like a very nice girl," my mom chimed in.

"I know. We can't wait for her to move here." Kaitlin agreed.

As we finished our pizza, the sun began to set.

"Well, I should get on the road. I've got a long drive ahead," my mom explained.

"I'll walk you out," I announced.

My mom and Kaitlin said their goodbyes, before I followed my mom out to her car.

All of the other parents had left, and the streets were filled with college students. Walking to and froe, as the parties were going to start soon.

"Thanks for staying and helping me get settled in," I stated, reaching out for a hug. My mom welcomed my embrace, pulling me in tightly.

"Of course, my girl." She smiled. "Ugh, the house is going to be so quiet again without you."

"I'm going to miss you too, mom." I started to choke.

She squeezed me tightly before letting me go and turning to get in the car. She pulled away from the curb and stuck her hand out the window, waving goodbye. I waved goodbye after her and let out a deep sigh, before heading back into the dorm.

I walked back into my room, to find Kaitlin had already changed into her pajamas.

"You read my mind," I teased her.

I changed into my sweats and climbed into my bottom bunk, pulling my comforter up to my chin. I turned out the light and rolled over onto my side when my phone chimed. I groaned and rolled back over to check the notification. It was a text message from Eric:

"Come outside"

I paused for a moment and stared at it, confused. I kicked off my blankets and slipped on my slippers, grabbing my key and heading for the door. I walked outside the front entrance to find Eric standing on the sidewalk with flowers in his hand. I stopped in my tracks. He was really there.

"Luna, I love you. I love you more than I knew was possible. I thought Colorado was more important, I thought it was something that I needed to explore now. But I was wrong. You're more important than my dream. You're more important than Colorado. I'll follow you anywhere. I'll get an apartment off campus so we can be here together while you complete school. I'll do whatever you want to do, Luna, because I'm in love with you," he professed.

I stood stunned, drinking in every word that escaped his lips. His perfectly shaped, cupid bow lips. I took in a deep inhale and ran down the front steps and jumped into his arms. He wrapped his hands around my waist and lifted me up into the air, spinning me around in a circle. I let out a squeal and wrapped my legs around his hips.

I leaned in and slammed my lips against his, eager to connect with lips. He kissed me back passionately, more intensely than any kiss we'd shared. This was it. He was the one, my Eric was here with me, finally ready to live happily ever after.

The
End

www.ingramcontent.com/pod-product-compliance
Lightning Source LLC
LaVergne TN
LVHW012019060526
838201LV00061B/4367